The Right Resolution
A Holiday Hearts Romance

Kristen Ethridge

Dear Reader

I t happens every 365 days.

The calendar flips to a new year. If you're like me, you'll keep writing the wrong date on all types of documents until February at the earliest.

Typically, people start diets, exercise plans, reading plans, going-back-to-church plans, actually using their planner plans, cleaning out their drawers plans, and a million other things that benefit from the jump-start that a clean slate gives.

There's just something about New Year's.

Last year, I made a giant vision board. I decided to strategically think about how I wanted my year to be.

If you're like me and you spend the month of December thinking about how you can make January different, then I think you'll see a lot of yourself in Eve Larson. Her past is holding her back, and she knows it—but she's got to make it through one last milestone on the calendar before she feels free to change and move forward.

Eve and Spencer's story is a little different than any other stories I've written. I've created more than one reunion romance—I love writing them. But Eve and Spencer were atypical. They knew each other. They had some history. They even had some trust issues. But they didn't have a relationship.

And from the moment Spencer shows up in the story, the fireworks aren't just for the New Year's sky at midnight. They're instantly attracted to each other as they are both looking for a reason to move past the common tie to their past.

As an author, it's fun when the characters take over the story. These two clearly knew who they were and what they wanted. And from the get-go, they wanted each other. But would ideas and people from their past prove to be a barrier? Or will they get past it and get the fresh start they each decided on?

I'd like to invite you to join me in Port Provident as we celebrate holidays and happily-ever-after this year with the Holiday Hearts series, set in my heartwarming small town of Port Provident, Texas.

All the best-

Kristen

PS... I'd like to invite you to become a part of my reader community today. Just go to www.kristenethridge.com/newsletter.[1]

One of my signature Sweet Escape Romances is Layla and Ridge's story, *A Place to Find Love*. Layla's spent her whole life searching for a greater meaning in her life. She comes to Port Provident running on fumes, but once she meets Ridge, she begins a journey that fills her with more than she ever

---

1. http://www.kristenethridge.com/newsletter

hoped for—faith, family, and a place to find the love she's always longed for. I'll send you a copy just for joining my reader community, plus you'll be able to keep up with the latest on my books and Port Provident through regular emails and more reader bonuses.

I promise these stories will lift you up and leave you with a smile.

One of the best ways to get to know Port Provident even better is to get your *Passport to Port Provident*. It's a behind-the-scenes reader exclusive that's available when you join me on Facebook Messenger[2].

www.kristenethridge.com[3]

Facebook[4] Instagram[5]

The Port Provident Reader[6] Society on Facebook

2.   https://m.me/KristenEthridgeBooks

3. http://www.kristenethridge.com

4. https://www.facebook.com/KristenEthridgeBooks

5. https://instagram.com/kristenethridge

6. https://www.facebook.com/groups/2422381554654795

Chapter One

"I thought I might find you here."

Eve Larson pulled her gaze reluctantly away from the rolling waves that stretched back toward the horizon. She hadn't heard that voice in a year, but it only took a split second and a syllable to take her mind back to another time, twelve months ago, in front of these same waves.

"Spencer. What are you doing here?"

She took a minute to size him up. He stood on the sand in a most un-beach outfit of moss green wool sweater, wide wale dark brown corduroy pants, and soft cocoa leather moccasins. Neat, clean, sharp. Typical Spencer.

Eve felt a faint tug of awareness and shook her head slightly, trying to clear the quickening rhythm from her pulse. The last time they'd spoken, it hadn't gone well.

"Eve? You okay?" The reflection of the waves showed in miniature in Spencer's green eyes.

She wished she wouldn't have looked up.

She wished she wouldn't have noticed.

But more than anything, she wished she wouldn't have cared.

"I'm fine. I'm just a little caught off guard." Eve turned back toward the waves. "What are you doing here? You didn't say."

"Same thing you are. Taking a few days off for the new year."

Eve's pulse began to race again, this time with the quick kindling of anger, not conditioned awareness. "You never take days off. And you could go anywhere in the world. Don't tell me that it's coincidence that you're standing in front of my mother's beach house in Port Provident, Texas, just by chance. You've thrown me a lot of lines, Spencer, but this time I'm not biting."

She squared her shoulders. No matter what he said, she would not turn her body, she would not turn her gaze. She would not give Spencer Canley another chance to tell her another tale.

Spencer took three steps, the sand giving a nearly soundless crunch under the soles of his expensive shoes. "I'm not trying to bait you."

"So what are you doing here?" Her patience was wearing thin. Spencer had intruded on her few days of hoped-for solitude, the days she'd planned to spend with a quiet focus on her future.

Not a focus on the white dress she should have been wearing.

Not a focus on the aisle she should have been walking down.

Not a focus on Spencer's brother, Mark, who should have been waiting there for her.

"It's not really a vacation, Eve, but you already figured that out."

She nodded. "So what is it?"

"I still work for Mark." He paused. "He asked me to bring you this envelope."

"A letter?" Eve turned, her disbelief overriding her resolve to stay still as a statue. "Mark and I are through. We've been through for a year. What more is there to do?"

Spencer reached in his back pocket and pulled out an envelope. A scowl pushed his brow into a furrow. He handed the paperwork to her slowly.

Eve reached her hand out, then hesitated. But there wasn't really any point. Mark Canley got what he wanted, when he wanted it. There weren't many people who would stand in his way. Not a brother. And certainly not the former love of his life.

Emphasis on *former*.

The paper felt cool and slightly damp to the touch. With a deep breath, she slid her finger in the gap on the envelope flap and tugged it open.

The letter was short and to the point. It didn't take more than a few seconds for Eve's eyes to scan the terse sentences Mark had scrawled in bold ink.

A lump like wet sand began to fill her throat. She tried to swallow it away, but her mouth had gone dry.

"He wants my ring back?" She almost didn't recognize the scratchy whisper as her own voice.

Spencer nodded. "He didn't let me see the contents of the letter first, but I wouldn't be surprised if that's what was in there. He's been talking about it for weeks."

"But...why?" She struggled a bit for the words.

Spencer pushed his hands into his pocket, then squared his own shoulders in much the same way Eve herself had only moments before when she first heard the voice from her past. "He's getting engaged. That's a one-of-a-kind stone, and he decided he wanted to reset it."

"But my mother helped him pick it out." Memories of the mother she lost to breast cancer too soon flooded into a mind already jumbled with too many thoughts.

"It's a stone that used to belong to the Russian imperial family. He doesn't care about the rest of it."

"He doesn't care about anything," Eve said into the wind. "Except himself."

Spencer didn't change position, just stood alongside Eve, as a brief gust kicked a wintry spray back on them both.

"I've known him my whole life, Eve. I used to idolize my older brother. But now? I'd say your assessment is correct."

"Come on," Eve said with a touch of resignation. "It's getting cold out here. The wind's picking up."

She turned around and began to walk back across the damp sand. Spencer followed in her wake, amazed by the calmness she displayed to the outside world. Did Eve ever show emotion? After a moment's shock, she seemed to just take it in stride, just like she did a year ago when Spencer was dispatched by Mark to break off the engagement between Eve and Mark.

Maybe being around Mark so long had hardened her heart to any emotion.

Spencer knew that had become true with him. And his recent understanding of that small, but damning fact helped him know he had to get out from under his brother's shadow and self-centered life. It had been a hard realization, since he'd spent most of his years on Earth believing the Canley brothers were tied by a bond of blood that couldn't be broken.

It had taken Spencer a while to figure out how to disengage without getting scorched by Mark's fire. The woman in front of him had gotten burned badly. It was a lesson Spencer had quietly taken to heart.

After walking up the stairs that ran along the side of the deck of the house held high on stilts, Eve slowly turned the key in the lock and opened the weathered door. The whole house seemed to have seen better days. The green paint had faded to a light lichen shade and a shutter was missing from the left side of one of the front windows.

Eve never seemed like the type to let herself go—or for that matter, anything she controlled. But maybe Spencer had been wrong about her taking everything as a matter of course. Maybe this year had been harder on his former almost-sister-in-law than he'd initially thought.

"I have it in the back room," she said without even turning around. "You can wait here if you'd like."

She gestured toward a striped couch, faded in a motley pattern by where the sun's rays had fallen through the window and sprayed across the fabric.

"You brought it with you for a weekend at the beach?" What woman carried her former engagement ring around when she traveled? Spencer's curiosity was piqued.

Eve stopped at the start of the short hallway and turned around. "As you noted, it's a unique stone." She pursed her lips tightly, their thin outline turning a bloodless white under the pressure. Then, without another word, she stepped down the hall and softly closed the bedroom door behind her.

Spencer looked around the room, buffeted by the silence around him. Only the wind outside howled. This time last year, he'd stood in the same room.

It seemed very different now, colder. Less cheerful.

Maybe it was just the weather. Outside the windows, storm clouds collected on the edge of the horizon and bunched up like a mass of black cotton balls filling the dusk sky.

A rumble of thunder shook the small beach house on its pilings. Spencer felt the wobble beneath his feet. He wished he hadn't put off coming down here to Eve's end of the island so long. Now it looked like he would get caught in a downpour.

Maybe that's what he needed, though, he thought dryly. Maybe a good, hard rain could wash away the guilt he felt about this trip and the last trip he'd made to Eve's little bungalow. Time certainly hadn't made the tightness in his throat go away.

Over the growl of the thunder and the splash of the oversized raindrops that landed with more force than a water balloon fight between children, he didn't hear Eve walk back into the room.

She held a chain delicately between two fingertips. The picture froze in his mind. The curve of her thumbnail, the clean glossy finish of the delicate shade of rose nail polish, the subtle twinkle of the thread-thin chain as it caught the glow of the light overhead.

Even though he'd told Eve he was running an errand for his boss, Spencer told *himself* this was a personal matter between two ex-lovers. Eve seemed to be returning it willingly. There wouldn't be conflict between her and Mark and that meant he wouldn't have to take sides—because he knew in his heart and his mind, he wouldn't be able to pick Mark's side.

But if she just gave it back at Mark's personal request, then, he could merely pretend to be nothing more than a courier between the two parties.

The diamond looked different than the last time Spencer saw it. A year ago, it rested snugly at the base of Eve's left ring finger, flanked by a wedge of smaller diamonds on either side. Now, it dangled at the end of the thin chain, surrounded by three pavé-style rings of sapphires. It was completely different, and yet, completely unmistakable.

The Kiss of Kiev. A three-carat circle of light and ice, given as part of a brooch made for the Empress Consort Maria Alexandrovna of Russia, to honor the birth of the Russian Grand Duchess Alexandra Alexandrovna in 1842. After the pretty, curly-headed blond died of meningitis at age six and her bereaved mother was moved to tears at the mention of her daughter's name, it was ordered packed away, where it was not recovered for several generations. Lost again after the death of the Russian imperial family at the hands of the Bolsheviks in 1917, it reappeared two years ago at Houston's finest estate broker. It was then bought by Mark Canley and at the time, the society pages that wrote about the ring and the engagement declared it to be a demonstration of his royal-sized love for his fiancée.

Perhaps, thought Spencer, anything the diamond touched was doomed to a dark end. The little Grand Duchess. The Romanovs themselves.

Mark's engagement to Eve.

Although this fool's errand made Spencer feel as muddied and awkward as the storm-drenched shoreline outside the living room window, maybe he was doing Eve a favor by removing it from her life.

Who knew what destruction it would witness next.

"Well, then, I suppose this is yours." Eve laid the stone on her palm and pushed it in Spencer's direction.

Lightning cracked outside and the raindrops unleashed with more ferocity than Spencer had seen in years. He couldn't help but feel this was some kind of sign that even Mother Nature disapproved of the deed he'd been put up to.

"Not mine. Mark's." Spencer didn't want to be in this any deeper than he already was.

"One and the same. You've done your brother's dirty work for years. You hide it behind that pretty title on your business card, but your hands are just as dirty as Mark's are, Spencer. You're cut from the same cloth." Her gaze locked on him like the point of a laser sight on a gun. "A self-absorbed, ruthless lot, the Canley brothers. Thank goodness your mother stopped after your younger brother. Houston would be overrun with any more of you."

Spencer stood still, too stunned to even put the precious stone into the tiny padded envelope he'd brought to keep it safe.

"You think I'm just like Mark?"

Eve gave a short, cutting laugh, then replied. "Of course I do. You're like two peas in a pod. The CEO of Canley Communications thinks up ways to run over people and the Senior Vice President of Operations carries them out. The

Canley brothers, always together. And always up to something."

Spencer looked down at the stone in his hand. The facets twinkled like broken icicles in a sphere of perfect glass. "He didn't ask for my advice or counsel beforehand. I'm just doing my job, Eve."

"Really? Is that what you tell yourself, Spencer? Because that's even worse. You do his dirty work and you don't have enough of a backbone to tell him no. I used to think you were different. I used to think I could trust you, but then last year..."

She tucked a lock of dark blonde hair behind her ear, running her fingers softly through the strands. Eve looked like she would blow over in a strong wind—like the downpour and gale that whipped around outside—but she never broke eye contact, never gave the slightest hint that she wasn't speaking with total conviction.

Except for that shy sweep of the hair. Taught to read the body language of others in a class he took for his MBA, Spencer knew exactly what that gesture meant.

He wanted to prove her wrong. And now he knew he could.

What he couldn't figure out is why, suddenly, it mattered so much for him to do so.

"I'm quitting. This is my last act of 'dirty work,' as you call it."

"Quitting? You've been your brother's shadow for a decade." Eve dropped her hand from her hair and cocked her head ever so slightly. "I don't believe it."

What Spencer didn't believe is that she could honestly think that. For a decade, he'd struggled to rein his brother in, like a wrangler with an unbroken horse. "It's just a job, Eve. You make it sound like I'm his partner in crime or something."

She raised her eyebrows ever so slightly.

"Not that there is any crime going on," Spencer gave a quick laugh, barely under his breath. "Just need to get that disclaimer out there."

Eve smiled gently, the upward turn of her lips transforming her whole face. It made her skin seem softer, her cheeks seem rounder, and her eyes more vibrantly catch what little light hadn't been overtaken by the storm.

Spencer couldn't help but stare a bit, mystified by the total transformation that could be brought by the movement of a few muscles.

"What?" The corners of Eve's smile dropped slightly lower.

He tried to wave it off. No way he wanted to tell Eve what he was really thinking. "Nothing."

The smile returned, this time broadly. She knew she had him in a corner. He could see she relished the moment. "Nothing always means something. Maybe I've spent more time with your brother than I have with you, but I've seen this look before. It's obviously genetic."

Her words mentally took the negotiator in Spencer to a boardroom. It was as though the other party had just gotten an admission of some key point to blow the whole carefully choreographed business dealing wide open.

Spencer had been exposed.

He didn't particularly like the feeling. It was...unusual.

But after tonight, he'd never see Eve again. He had what he came for, cool and slick in his hand. He fingered the stone. It felt as solid as the hardball Eve was playing right this second.

He'd never see her again. She'd been pushed out of his brother's life, and once he got in the car and drove back down Provident Island's main highway, Eve Larson would be out of Spencer's life as well. So, it wouldn't hurt to give her the answer she wanted. He'd already taken so much from her anyway.

"I was looking at your smile." Spencer threw it out there, matter-of-factly, just to see what she'd do with the truth.

"My smile?" As he'd suspected, she didn't see the truth coming. She probably expected some veiled sarcasm. That's what Mark would have dished out.

"It's the truth."

Eve fiddled with a lock of her hair, self-confidence creeping in and stripping some of that sassiness that had filled her face only moments ago.

"The truth." The short syllables came out soberly.

"Yes, the truth, Eve. You're pretty when you smile. Hasn't anyone ever told you that before?" Spencer could feel the crack and waver of her self-confidence, like the watery landscape outside after one of the lightning strikes made contact from the sky.

Eve didn't know what to do with the compliment from him, that much was clear.

He couldn't turn off the analytical side of his brain.

Couldn't stop himself from going down a rabbit trail of wondering why.

Couldn't stop himself from reaching out to still the movement as she tried to shake her head no, to help her understand he was right and her hesitance was misplaced.

Spencer's hands fell on the gentle curve of Eve's shoulders. His right hand connected with the simple cotton of her striped shirt. His left hand, still holding the diamond, landed on the soft skin exposed by the wide boatneck-style collar.

He'd known Eve for years. He'd shaken her hands in greeting, given her brotherly hugs goodbye at the end of dinner parties, and probably come in contact with her in a hundred other small, casual ways. But never had he touched her bare skin and lingered.

Never had he felt the softness of her pale, creamy skin under his fingers.

Never had he wanted more.

Eve raised her gaze to Spencer's. She wasn't smiling now.

Her lips parted, a hesitant breath floating between them.

"Do you need anything else?" Her words were barely louder than the steady pounding of the rain on the cottage roof and windows.

Yes, he did.

But how did Spencer tell her he needed her to understand that though he shared genetics and office space with his brother, he wasn't cut from the same cloth as Mark—that her assumptions were wrong?

It seemed simple, and to want her to understand was probably silly.

But it was as real to him as the measured movements of his finger touching her collarbone, as her chest expanded and retreated with each inhale and exhale.

He thought about the diamond between them, clear and flawless. Fit for royalty.

And what was he?

Only fit to do his brother's dirty work, according to the woman in front of him.

He needed to leave, before he tried even more to convince her otherwise.

So there was only one way to answer her softly-spoken question—did he need anything else?

"No. I don't."

Spencer slid his hands off Eve's shoulders, allowing himself a few more undeserved seconds of silk and diamonds under his fingertips.

"Then I guess you'd better go." Eve looked at Spencer with unsure eyes. Clearly, she didn't know what to make of the touch or of the moment, either. "You have everything you need."

He had the Kiss of Kiev, the diamond he needed.

But looking at Eve, remembering his touch on her skin and the slight sigh on her lips, he knew one thing for certain.

He didn't have everything he wanted.

Chapter Two

The rain blew straight back, flinging droplets into the beach house as Spencer opened the door and fought his way out. Eve heard the thump of his footsteps down the wooden stairs that ran along the side of the house. The older house sat about fourteen feet off the ground on pilings, as all the homes in this quiet beach community did. There was no cover over the stairs, so Spencer was probably getting soaked with each step.

Eve didn't care.

She briefly chided herself for her callousness, but thought about her diamond in his pocket—the diamond her mother helped Mark pick out. Losing Mark didn't hurt in the same way that losing that diamond did, and not because it was a gemstone worth more than every other asset she had combined, several times over.

Anna Larson would never see her only daughter as a bride. She'd never see her only daughter become a mother. But even as breast cancer ripped apart her body, cannibalizing her strength and substance from the inside, Anna had pulled herself out of bed to join Mark for one day of shopping to pick out the perfect ring of promise for Eve.

Anna never left her bed again, and died four days shy of a month later. But Eve could still feel her gentle care every time she looked at that beautiful sparkling circle, set in that delicate platinum setting. It was why, when Mark decided he didn't want Eve's love in his life any more, she took the ring and had it reset into a pendant surrounded by her mother's favorite sapphire stones, where it would hang close to her heart. In some small way, she could keep Anna—along with her bravery and her love—there with her always.

And now Anna was gone and the stone was gone, and there was nothing Eve could do to make either of them come back.

A knock sounded at the door, breaking Eve's trail of memories.

She opened it carefully, shielding herself behind the door and away from the force-driven rain. Spencer stood in front of her, as soaked as though he'd been through a full wash cycle.

"Can I come in?" He pushed water back as it ran from the front of his hair down over his eyes.

Eve stood back and opened the door wide enough to let him in, her feelings about the last hour at war with her common decency. "What happened?"

"Did you know the parking area under your house floods pretty easily?"

Eve nodded. "Well, sure, you're sitting at sea level. The road's been raised a little higher and so everything runs down below the houses."

"Well, I wish I had a beach-ready, nice tall Jeep like yours down there. Because when you have a low-profile sports car, the equation of below sea level plus downpour presents a problem. The water's probably over a foot deep down there, just standing like a swimming pool. It's barely over the bottom of the doors.

There's water inside my car. And I guess there's some water in something important, because my car refuses to start."

"Serves you right." Eve mumbled.

"I heard that."

"I kind of hoped you would." Eve couldn't keep her face smooth and impressionless as she spoke. The wry smile tugging on her lips came through in each syllable.

"Why?" Spencer didn't move from the small tiled entry area, water puddling all around him.

"Because it's the truth, and it's deliciously ironic." Eve turned and began to walk through the small house, still talking. "You came here to do your brother's dirty work, but you can't make your quick getaway. That's how Mark likes to do things—get in, get out, leave the mess behind."

"Eve." His voice rose to a shout, carrying to the back corner of the house where she dug in a closet. "I'm not Mark."

She walked back into the living room, then stopped, caught by the sight of Spencer. She hadn't really looked at him when she let him back inside, but now couldn't help but size him up. The soft leather moccasin-style shoes were soaked through, and there was a healthy splatter of water on the corduroy pants, soaking them to about midway up the calf. And then, the sweater caught her attention and wouldn't let go.

The moss green color had turned almost black as it soaked up the rainwater, and it had gone slightly stiff as it molded the fine gauge of cashmere to a set of broad, rounded shoulders, across Spencer's chest, and down his abdomen. The wet wool clung to him like a second skin, outlining chiseled definitions and making Eve see Spencer in a way she never had before.

He'd been Mark's brother, and while he'd been good-looking in that same polished way of all the Canley brothers, she'd never allowed herself to really study him or think about him as anything but her future brother-in-law—because that would have been more than just a little bit weird and completely uncalled for.

But now... he wasn't her future brother-in-law. He wasn't anything with a connection to her. The fragmented thoughts in her mind at this moment were definitely not sisterly.

She aimed squarely at Spencer's mid-section as she threw a soft blue bath towel. She needed to take action before her those thought fragments took over everything rational in her mind.

"Thanks." Spencer leaned over and towel-dried his hair, then tried to blot and squeeze as much of the wet as he could out of the sweater and the pants. With his toes, he kicked off the leather shoes, then pushed them toward the door and out of the way.

"You still look like a drowned rat." Maybe if she thought of Spencer as a very wet rodent, she wouldn't be tempted to think about how that sweater molded perfectly to his chest.

"Coincidentally, that's pretty much how I feel." He plucked at the lightweight wool sleeve. "Bitterly cold and soaked to the bone. But I'm not sure what else I can do about it."

He held the towel back out toward Eve. "Thanks for the towel. I think it helped. But I'm too wet to really know for sure."

"Maybe I've got something else that can help. Give me a second."

Eve wadded up the wet towel and tossed it in a chair as she walked back down the short hallway. Once she got to the guest room, she opened up the small closet and leaned inside, looking toward the far right corner.

They were there, still hanging in the same spot where they'd been for longer than she cared to remember—a pair of jeans and a button-down shirt Mark had left behind. She'd almost given them to Goodwill twenty times in the last twelve months, but she kept putting it off. She justified her procrastination by telling herself she would put them in with a big donation of Anna's clothes and other household goods instead of taking a few items at a time.

But she'd never quite had the heart or the strength to give away her mother's possessions—not yet, at least—and so, Mark's leftover outfit had continued to hang in the back corner of the closet, almost forgotten.

In all the times she'd thought about donating the jeans and shirt to someone in need, she never imagined that person would be Spencer Canley.

"Do you think these will fit?" She brought the outfit over to the small three-by-three square of tile flooring near the door where Spencer continued to stand and drip.

"What's this?" Spencer reached for the jeans, holding them away from his own soaked pair of pants.

"Some old jeans and a shirt of Mark's that he left here ages ago. Y'all are about the same size, aren't you?"

"Yeah, more or less. Thanks, Eve. Do you have somewhere I can change?"

A pang twisted ever-so-slightly in her chest. She realized she was going to miss the visual effects of that soaking wet sweater. "Down the hall, second door on the left."

"Great. Thanks." Spencer nodded, then stepped gingerly off the tile and onto the hardwood flooring.

With the click of the bathroom door behind him, Eve was alone with her thoughts for a moment. She didn't know what to make of the last hour or so of her life.

Spencer Canley had walked back onto her beach, reminding her of a hurt she'd spent a year trying to shake off. She was legally ordered to surrender a possession that she'd had re-crafted to symbolize a connection to her mother. She'd seen Spencer and her diamond walk out the door, only to walk right back in.

And she'd caught herself staring at Spencer with more intensity than she'd probably ever stared at her ex-fiancé.

What a mess. All of it.

She didn't *want* to notice the way the wet weave of the wool fit Spencer like a second skin—in much the same way she didn't *want* to give him her diamond necklace—but in both cases, what she wanted didn't matter. She couldn't fight back against Mark Canley's legal demands. And she didn't want to fight back against noticing Spencer Canley's chiseled good looks. Just once, she wanted to do something completely irresponsible and not care about the consequences.

And Spencer Canley fit that bill about as good as that sweater fit him.

The rain continued to pour outside, limiting Spencer's chances of leaving any time soon. He had a dead car downstairs and his very presence reminded her she had a dead heart. Maybe they did have something in common, after all.

Eve sighed. Neither she nor Spencer were going anywhere, figuratively or literally.

Too bad Eve's troubles weren't as easily fixed as a stalled-out sports car.

Spencer walked back in the living room. He'd left the red plaid shirt with a faint white stripe untucked over a pair of dark wash jeans. Eve remembered the outfit so well, but on Spencer, it seemed completely new, just from the way he carried himself.

"Look, Eve...I know you wish you could get rid of me right now." Spencer folded his wet clothes and sat them next to the ruined pair of leather shoes beside the door. "I did want to say I'm sorry things worked out like this."

She sat on the couch and pushed herself back into a corner, against the faded red stripes of the cushions. "It just is what it is, I guess."

"I was thinking, though, it doesn't necessarily have to be." He sat on an overstuffed chair across from her.

"What do you mean? You've got the engagement ring. What else is there?"

"I don't know, exactly. But it's almost New Year's. A time for new beginnings. I know I've delivered some bad news to you, more than once." He hesitated, as though he wanted to get the words right. "And the only thing I can say to you is that I'm sorry for my role in that."

Eve hadn't fully processed Spencer's reappearance in her life and what had happened this afternoon. His apology added to that list of things to work through. It left her feeling even more confused than just moments ago.

"Did I say something wrong?" Spencer looked at Eve, and she saw his eyes take on a spark of compassion. He was trying to follow her train of thought.

"I don't know how to explain it to you without understanding it myself."

His hand gestured at the window, still being slapped without mercy by the driving rain. "I think we've got some time. My car isn't going to dry out any time soon. Take whatever time you need."

"Time? You know, Spencer, time doesn't just magically fix everything." Immediately, her mind filled with thoughts of the hurt that took over her heart like a blackened bruise every time she thought about Anna's death. Or the cold shock she still felt when she thought about her engagement ending.

And she knew she'd never forget how when Spencer followed her onto the sand today, both of those life-altering feelings were brought back to the forefront of her mind in an unavoidable way.

"I know, Eve, believe me, I know." He inadvertently sprayed the table between them with a light sheen of water droplets as he briefly nodded in agreement.

"Do you, really?" Eve heard hard steel in her words. "Your mother's still alive. Your engagement wasn't broken by some proxy. Your New Year's weekend of reflection hasn't been shattered by the surprise appearance of some guy on a sand dune behind you."

Spencer didn't hesitate before spitting back his reply.

"My mother's a society queen who doesn't give regard to anything but herself. I've never had a broken engagement because I work twenty-four-seven at my brother's beck and call. I don't have time to date someone, much less marry them. And although my coming here wasn't a surprise to *me*, that didn't make it any less difficult to carry out. I didn't want to be here today, Eve."

She didn't necessarily blame him for answering with some defensiveness, but she wasn't prepared to give on this. He didn't have the first clue what her recent life had been like, as first Anna, then Mark—the people who were supposed to love her unconditionally forever—left. Yes, they'd left for very different reasons—one due to cancer, the other for...well, callousness, Eve supposed. But no matter the reason, the outcome was the same.

She'd been left alone, and it hurt.

In fact, it hurt so much that sometimes it left her unable to breathe or to understand how everything had gone so, so wrong in so short a time.

"Why would it be difficult for you, Spencer? You walked in and handed me a demand letter. How hard is that?" Her heart rate sped up a little bit as she pressed him. Whatever he thought he'd been through, she knew there was no way it could compare to the events that had come her way lately.

Spencer had no right to act like he'd walked in shoes like hers. And Eve felt compelled to make him understand it.

He took in a deep breath and clenched his jaw slightly. "Because I think Mark's wrong. I thought he was wrong a year ago and I think he's wrong about sending me here today."

Eve turned slightly so she could stare out the window and avoid looking in Spencer's direction.

"Then why'd you do it?" She followed one drop of rain as it slid from the top of the window to the bottom of the sill, then started the visual game over again with another droplet.

"I was just doing my job, Eve. I told you that earlier." He hesitated. "But that doesn't mean I agree with what Mark does. I rarely agree with what Mark does these days."

"And so you're leaving your job?"

"Yes, I am. Our other brother David left Canley Communications a few months ago. Mark's always pushed the limits, you know. But he's made some deals with some defense contractors in the Middle East that I don't think are right. He's gotten rich by being the first guy to come in and bring his breed of technology to the corners of the world no one wants to play in. And now that he's hooked up with some of these leaders of these former Russian republics on his latest project, well, he's become a bully. There's not much I can do to change his mind, but I can stand up for what I know is right. And that means I can't be his second-in-command anymore. I'm not going to be made to feel uncomfortable in my own office, not even for my own brother."

Eve digested Spencer's explanation. She didn't want to know more about what shenanigans Mark was up to in tiny corners of the world. She felt like it was better not to ask for the answers to the questions which had already popped into her head.

Well, all of them except one.

"So he's engaged again?" Eve forced the words past the lump in her throat. As long as she didn't look right at Spencer, she could ask the question that she knew wouldn't leave her mind unless she learned the answer.

"He is. To the daughter of the oligarch he's working on this latest project with. Dimitri Moldayev. That's why he wants your diamond back. He bought it for you because it was special, unique. He wants to give it to her because of the history. He wants to impress her father and become rich beyond his wildest dreams."

As much as Eve told herself she wouldn't care, no matter what Spencer's answer was, that got her attention. "Wait. Svetlana Moldayeva? That's Mark's fiancée?"

"You know her?"

"I read a lot of those glossy magazines they sell at the supermarket. They're my guilty pleasure. How's that for irony? To make myself feel better after getting dumped, I read gossip magazines about fancy people around the world, and then I find out the man who dumped me is engaged to an heiress who shows up in those magazines—famous solely because her daddy's rich."

Eve began to laugh. The little hiccups took her breath away and the full weight of that irony settled in her chest, transforming the dry laugh into chokes that tried in vain to hold back tears.

Spencer got up from his chair and without a word sat next to Eve and placed his arm around her. Earlier, when he'd put his hands on her shoulders, it had been a surprise and she'd been unable to really sort out how she felt about it. Now, his muscled forearm felt comforting, steady. Like the support she'd been looking for to keep her from falling face-first into her own emotions.

But why did the support she'd hoped for have to come from Spencer? Why did she have to lean on the arm of the man who'd delivered most of the news that had brought her to tears in the first place?

He squeezed her shoulder with his right hand and gently placed the first finger of his left hand under her chin and tilted it up.

His green eyes were dark, the irises gone almost the same color as the pupil. "She's only rich in money, Eve. I know you. You're rich in heart."

Eve swallowed hard. "Not anymore."

Spencer lifted his right hand and gently tucked a stray lock of hair behind her ear, then smoothed again to secure it. The brush of his finger felt soft as a whisper as it traced the top curve of cartilage. Her breath came short, cutting off the life from the quiet sobs and turning the emotion in her veins into something else resembling the steady pop of carbonation. It would be too easy to lose herself in the simplicity of the moment.

Spencer's finger pressed and Eve looked back into his eyes, then tried to pull back. She needed to search that gaze and remember. She needed to remember who he was and what part he'd played in her life.

That was the only way she'd keep herself from more hurt.

Spencer shifted and dropped his finger, then pulled his arm back to himself, the cotton of his borrowed sleeve sliding across the thin knit of her own cotton shirt like the glide of a ballroom dance, deceiving in carefully-choreographed simplicity.

Eve wondered if Spencer knew what was running through her mind and her veins.

"I'm sorry, Evie." The words came out as though wrapped around sandpaper.

No one had ever called her Evie before.

She wanted to hear it again. But she knew she couldn't.

She wanted more. But she knew she shouldn't.

Spencer was only inches away, and she could still feel something. Hopefully it was nothing more than static electricity, nothing more than a crackle between two socks in a dryer. She couldn't wrap her head around it being a spark between two people who had no business being together. Eve waited for her breath to settle back to a normal pattern, but he started to speak again, and that made it tough for her to focus.

"You were right, you know."

"I was right?" The breathless moment fell apart, broken as Eve tried to use logic to figure out to what Spencer was referring.

"I did my brother's dirty work. And you deserved better." His weight pushed in the fluff of the center couch cushion. "You still do."

"Spencer..."

He cut her off, and she was glad, because she didn't know exactly where she was going with that.

"Look, I think we're going to be here a while. The rain shows no signs of stopping. I really hate to impose, but as long as the rain is standing down there, the water is just adding to my insurance claim and car repair bill. I can call a cab if you want me to go."

She'd planned on a solitary New Year's Eve weekend. A passage of time where she could reflect on the transition, take inventory of the things that had happened in the last year and give them their due so she could finally break free of the holding pattern she felt she'd been in for far too long.

But now, she could still smell the damp of Spencer's hair and feel the phantom presence of his touch on her chin and her ear, and she wanted to revise her plans. She wanted him to stay. He knew what she'd been through. He'd been a part of it. Maybe he was what she needed to clear the air of the past. Maybe then she could move on and make a real start for the next year.

Maybe Spencer had been brought back into her life for a reason. Eve didn't believe in coincidences. Through everything in the last year, she hadn't lost the belief that all things could be made right.

"No, you can stay. It'll be better than last New Year's, right?"

She tried to laugh the small pang of nervousness off.

"I promise it will. I owe that much to you." Spencer smiled, a sincere grin that made that pang soften like butter left on the counter. "What's in your kitchen?"

"My kitchen?" Considering the last few minutes, that definitely wasn't where Eve saw this conversation going.

"Why don't you go do something nice for yourself, like take a warm bath and read one of those gossip magazines for an hour? I'll pull together something for dinner."

"You don't need to do that, Spencer."

"I know I don't, Evie. I want to."

He said her name like that again. Her heart warmed a little at the sound of it. And against her better judgment, she trusted that Spencer Canley meant what he said.

But while Spencer might know what he wanted right now—to cook dinner—Eve didn't trust that she knew her own mind.

Or her own heart.

Eve closed the door to her small bedroom and leaned against it, eyes closed, as her mind raced. After a few deep breaths, she knew she needed to make a phone call. She needed to know if she was crazy or not. Amanda would give it to her straight.

Eve's hand shook a bit as she picked the phone up off the table and dialed the number that would connect her to her good friend who was working the gallery this weekend as a favor to Eve while she took some time away.

"Hey there. How's your New Year's retreat going?" Amanda Marsh answered the phone with her usual dose of sunshine in her voice.

"Can you talk a minute?"

"Sure. I just locked up the gallery. I sold your big sunset today. It's headed down your way, to sit in a beach house down on the island."

That seemed fitting. The sunset painting had been inspired by evenings here on the Gulf of Mexico, so it seemed appropriate that it would return to the coast. At least that was one thing she felt sure of today.

But she had to get her best friend's counsel on the major uncertainty that had come into her life today. "Spencer Canley is here."

"Mark's brother?" The skepticism came through the line clearly, even though the phone connection down at the coast could sometimes be fickle.

"Yes." Eve heaved the lone word out on a sigh.

"Why? He came to the beach house? That makes no sense, Eve."

Her friend didn't know how right she was. "Nothing makes any sense, Amanda. He came here to collect the diamond from my old engagement ring. He delivered some fancy letter full of legal words ordering me to surrender it. Mark wants it back because he's getting engaged again—you remember the history on the ring right?"

"How could I forget? He bought you some queen's ring. It was cool at the time—before he became a total jerk."

"It belonged to Russian royalty, yes. Anyway, he's getting engaged to some Russian socialite now and he wants to give her the Kiss of Kiev to impress her family. So he sent Spencer down here to get it."

Eve flopped herself down on the bed, legs hanging over the edge.

"And you said Spencer's still there?"

"Yes. In the kitchen. Making me dinner. It's pouring down rain and it flooded and now his little sports car won't start."

Amanda gave an edgy laugh, honed in her day job of teaching English to high school students here in Port Provident. "Wait. He came to take back your priceless diamond and now he's stuck there and making you dinner? Just when I thought your dealings with the Canley brothers couldn't get any weirder."

Eve sighed again, unable to formulate any better way of communicating her feelings.

"But?" Amanda read right through Eve's wordlessness.

"It gets weirder than even that." Eve squirmed a bit as she fought the reality of what she was going to have to admit.

"How could this story get any more messed up?"

"I'm having thoughts about Spencer Canley. I'm hiding out in the bedroom trying to figure out what's going on with me. You're my best friend. You have to help me."

"You're...having...thoughts?" Amanda dragged out the sentence. "Seriously, Eve. Just come out and say it."

Eve looked around the room, as though Spencer might be hiding in a corner. However, the sound of cabinet doors shutting in the kitchen confirmed he was still where she left him. She lowered her voice.

"I think...IthinkSpencerCanleyiskindahot." She rushed the words out on a breathless, quick whisper.

"You what? Say that again."

Eve's heart rate quickened, and she battled it as she tried to speak more clearly. "I think Spencer Canley is hot. I caught myself checking out his sweater. And, for a split second, I swear I thought about kissing him."

"Yeah, hun, still can't hear you."

She knew good and well Amanda heard her the last time. "You're baiting me."

"Maybe. But it's kind of fun." Amanda paused. "And it keeps me from laughing."

Eve drummed her heels against the frame of the bed. "Why are you laughing at me?"

"Because you're the only person I know this could happen to. So...what are you going to do about it?"

Eve sat straight up on the bed and her voice was no longer tucked into a whisper. "I don't know. That's why I'm calling you!"

"Eve? Are you yelling? Is everything ok in there?" Spencer's voice shouted from the kitchen.

"Yes, I'm fine." Eve raised her voice and replied, then lowered it back. "Except that I'm not. Talk me out of this, Amanda."

The voice back in Houston shot her reply through the phone quickly and clearly. "Nope."

"Some help you are," Eve mumbled.

"I *am* trying to help you."

Eve wasn't buying it. She felt every bit as confused as she did when she first picked up the phone. "How so?"

"You said you were going down there to change your life this weekend, right?"

"Yes, but I just meant I was making changes for the new year. You know, like how people decide to start going to the gym in January. I was just going to make some resolutions, in the vein of 'quit thinking about the past and move forward in the present.' Spencer Canley is the past."

"Clearly you have him mistaken for Mark Canley." Eve could hear the chiding in Amanda's voice.

"No, I don't. I was supposed to be marrying Mark tomorrow. I know the difference between the two. But Spencer's the one who actually broke off the engagement. He's the one who asked for the ring back."

"Why don't you quit overthinking it? I'm sure his car is going to start soon and he'll be on his merry way. In the meantime, why don't you not worry about something that hasn't happened—and probably won't happen? Sufficient to the day is the evil thereof. Or something like that. I think that's how the Bible verse goes."

Amanda made way too much sense—probably another trait she picked up by teaching high schoolers all day. Someone had to rise above all the hormones in the halls of Port Provident High.

Eve and Spencer were grown adults with a complex history. Besides, just because she couldn't help but notice him didn't mean he had the same issue with her. After all, she wasn't wearing a soaking wet wool sweater plastered to her every curve.

"You're right. I hate saying it, but you're always right."

"I know. It's a gift and a burden." Amanda laughed dramatically.

"I'm just going to go take my bubble bath and get ready for dinner." Eve walked into the bathroom and pulled a towel off the rack, then laid it gently next to the tub. She turned both taps on the tub and began to let it fill.

"That's my girl. Ok, I have to go finish closing up the gallery." Amanda paused. "Promise me this, though."

"What?" Eve looked at her reflection in the mirror. Her hair fell loose down on to her shoulders and her face was free of makeup. There was no way Spencer had taken note of her in the same way she had of him. All would be well.

"If he does try to kiss you, don't overthink it. Make a resolution in favor of kissing."

"Aaugh. You are no help. Bubble bath, take me away." Eve slipped a toe in the water, testing the temperature.

"Hey, there's nothing wrong with a few fireworks. It is New Year's, after all."

Amanda disconnected the call before Eve could reply. But perhaps it was just as well. The pounding of her pulse had finally slowed. Spencer Canley was only looking for one kiss—the Kiss of Kiev diamond. He certainly wasn't looking for a kiss from his brother's ex-fiancé.

That would be crazy.

And the only crazy person here was her—the one who'd shut herself off from the world like a Hobbit. This confirmed it. It was time to get out and live her life so her imagination could quit running away with her.

As an artist, she appreciated imagination. But there was such an idea as too much of a good thing. Especially when it came to Spencer Canley.

And his soaking wet sweater.

Spencer felt a little awkward as he opened the small pantry, looking for some ingredients to use for dinner. He was dressed in his brother's old clothes, in a home with his brother's ex-fiancée, and stuck there less than twenty-four hours away from what should have been his brother's wedding day. Some difficult thoughts weighed heavily on his mind. He couldn't even imagine what raced through Eve's head. When he announced his presence out there on the sand, he'd probably interrupted a very personal moment, something much deeper than just a walk on the beach.

He opened a box of bowtie pasta and poured it into a pot of boiling water, then tossed in a small handful of salt and stirred. Watching the small twists percolate among the bubbles made him think about the twists and turns in his own life of late.

A jaunty tune broke the stillness around Spencer. His cellphone vibrated on the table in the living room where he'd set it earlier.

Spencer looked at the face of his smartphone and didn't really want to answer. But he didn't have much choice. Until he officially turned in his resignation when he returned to the office on January third, he was still on the Canley Communications payroll. And that meant he answered the phone when the CEO called.

Even if he was coming to despise the callous worldview of Mark Canley more with each passing minute.

Spencer tapped the green button on the face of the phone. "Hey, Mark."

"Do you have it?" Mark didn't waste any syllables, that was for sure.

"In my pocket." He glanced at the soaked pile of clothes laying by the door.

"Good. When will you be back? Fortner's Jewelry is open until eight tonight. You can just drop it off there. They know what to do with it."

Typical Mark. Grand plans made...for someone else to execute.

"I won't be there tonight, Mark."

The sound of Mark's voice became hard as the diamond in question. "Why not? They're closed tomorrow for New Year's Eve. I need this for the reception at the Consulate on the sixth. You need to get there tonight."

"I can't." Spencer reminded himself this was the last time he'd ever get bossed around by his brother like this. It helped him bite his tongue.

"Find a way. Where are you?"

"I'm still on Provident Island."

"Then get off Provident Island. This isn't hard, Spencer. Pay your tab at wherever you are and get going. You have just enough time to get there."

Spencer couldn't possibly make Mark any more angry than he was at this moment, so he decided not to hedge. "I'm at Eve's beach house. It's pouring down rain here. Everything's flooded and my car is stalled out. I'm not going anywhere for the foreseeable future."

"You always did like living in my shadow, Spence. Too bad you've got to go. You might have gotten lucky, consoling her over her lost wedding day." Mark gave a mirthless laugh, full of bite and self-importance. "Now, figure out a way to get your car started and get back to Houston."

His jaw clenched slightly, listening to Mark speak about Eve like she was a cast-off.

Spencer liked to do everything by the book, preferred for things to be outlined in clear language. Contracts made him feel secure. Handing his brother a formal letter of resignation was going to check that box for him. But maybe there was a time to throw the book out and just act.

And maybe this was that time.

As he listened to another of Mark's short, abrasive laughs, Spencer *knew* this was the time. He wasn't going to live in his brother's shadow anymore and he wasn't going to jump through any hoops to return this diamond to him.

"No, Mark. It's not going to happen." Spencer threw it out there. No going back. No waiting until January third.

"Not going to happen?" Mark wasn't laughing now. "She's my ex-fiancée. That's my property and you work for me. You do what I say."

"Not anymore." Though he knew he was in the midst of not just a rainstorm, but now also a maelstrom of a completely different type, Spencer felt an ease as he said the definitive words.

"What?" Mark practically spit out his response.

"I don't work for you anymore. Eve deserves better than an ex-fiancé like you. And I deserve a brother who doesn't use me to do his dirty work."

"Spencer, you're going to regret this." It sounded like Mark was gritting out the words.

Spencer knew better than to cross his brother, but as his right-hand for almost a decade, he knew of more skeletons in Mark's closet than he could even begin to count. The timing may have been rash, but the decision wasn't, and Spencer wasn't backing down.

"I'll be the judge of that."

"Oh there will be a judge alright. You're breaching your contract, Spencer."

"Texas is an at-will employment state, Mark. Either you or I can end our employment relationship at any time, for any reason. Besides, dear brother, I never signed a contract with any language like that. I gave the final approval on all your contracts, remember?" He paused, hearing a rustle in the other room. "I may be living in your shadow, as you put it, but I'm still my own man. I'm not that stupid."

And it was time to end this call and get on with being that man, far away from the pretentious influence of Mark Canley.

"This isn't over, Spencer."

"It is. And so is this call, Mark. Happy New Year."

Spencer pulled the phone away from his ear and deliberately pressed the red bar on the screen with his thumb, cutting off his brother and his former life.

He didn't know exactly what he'd be doing going forward, but keeping the pot of pasta from boiling over seemed like a good start.

"Spencer?" Eve came into the kitchen behind him, clad in a pair of worn jeans and a gray collegiate sweatshirt. Her hair was wound tightly inside of a towel perched on her head like a topping of meringue on a pie.

He saw her hazel eyes, sparkling like glassy topaz and he drank in the sight of her like she was a flute of champagne waiting for tomorrow night. He'd seen her in evening gowns at cocktail parties for the firm and bathing suits as she vacationed at resorts in the Mexican Riviera with Mark, but he'd never seen her look more beautiful than right now.

"Dinner's almost ready. I hope pasta is ok. I found some noodles and sauce in the pantry and there was lettuce in the fridge, along with some other things to make a salad."

"That sounds wonderful." She paused and reached up to twirl a lock of hair again, a sign Spencer now recognized as a manifestation of some nervousness, but instead brushed the sky blue terrycloth of the towel on her head. "Um...was that Mark you were talking to?"

"I tried to get off the phone before you overheard that." He wondered how much she'd caught.

"So it was Mark?"

Although he was about two minutes out from the termination of his employment at Canley Communications, he knew one thing for certain—he didn't want to hide behind any more smoke and mirrors. He wanted to let his yes be *yes* and his no be *no*.

"It was. He called me."

"And then you quit your job?"

"I told you I was going to. Now just happened to be a better time than waiting for the new year." Spencer turned away, using a need to check the pasta as an excuse to duck for a brief moment. Not much longer on the noodles. He opened cabinets, searching for something to drain the bowties with and found a colander, then sat it in the sink to wait.

Eve followed behind him and began to pull plates out of the cabinet. Although she was small of stature, her presence filled the room. He could feel it pressing against him, reminding Spencer she was there. Reminding him that he'd been there for some of the biggest wrongs in her life.

Reminding him of the thought he couldn't get out of his head—maybe the lead-up to this New Year's Eve would be the time for him to right some of those wrongs. Maybe it wasn't coincidence that he was here, now.

"You said you'd be the judge about something." Eve opened a cabinet and grabbed two glasses, then turned to Spencer with a shy smile. "Now, what did you mean?"

"Oh, that? Just a little bit of contract law." He didn't want to get her hopes up before he formulated a plan.

He'd always been risk-averse.

But that stopped five minutes ago.

Eve walked past again, coming back in the narrow galley kitchen for silverware. He should have moved out of her way.

He certainly shouldn't have reached out his hand.

And he had no explanation for why he reached up and loosened the twist of the blue towel covering her hair and gently lifted it off, then dropped it to the ground. It made a muted sound as it made contact with the tile, much like the continued steady slap of the rain on the windows.

A roll of thunder growled low outside as Spencer threaded his fingers through the twisted curls that fell just over Eve's shoulders. Damp, they looked as dark as a chocolate bar instead of their usual honey-and-toast coloring.

Eve locked her topaz stare on him, telling him without so much as a single word that she wasn't moving away.

Spencer reached through the curls and brushed his fingers against the soft curve of her neck, then slid his hand around to cup the base of her head.

Eve placed her fingers lightly on his forearm. One, two, three, four, five fingertips hesitantly touched Spencer's skin, their gentle graze burning his skin like feathers on fire.

He felt a charge of awareness as instinct began to take over. He'd stood feet away from numerous women before, about to lean in. He'd always thought he'd been perfectly normal, getting caught in the moment and not holding back. But never before had he wanted not simply more, but so much more.

He wanted to know the taste of Eve's kiss. He wanted to know if she closed her eyes. He wanted to know who was on the other side of the tawny gemstone gaze.

He wanted the risk. All the years spent being steady and cautious. They were gone. He felt something in the air, and with each breath, he could feel himself taking in a little more of whatever it was.

Jagged flashes of lightning crackled and reflected in the windows. He caught a glimpse of sparkle and light in the centers of Eve's eyes. She came a little closer. Did she feel it too? Was she testing the space between them?

A hiss filled the air, tangled with the other sounds, and only then did Eve rock back on her heel.

"Oh no," she said softly, and Spencer's adrenaline broke with a crack that he felt in his veins. "The pasta. It's boiling over."

So was Spencer, but he had no choice but to lower his hands as Eve took a step back and then over to the stove, where she turned off the burner, and carried the pasta to the sink. The water sluiced through the colander with a hiss, taking the charged moment between Spencer and Eve along with it.

Chapter Three

Eve didn't want to feel like the pasta's exuberance had saved her from something, but she knew the semolina had rescued her.

From what, exactly, though? From Spencer Canley? From a kiss?

From finally feeling like she was desirable after a year of feeling like a piece of trash left behind on the curb?

The whole tone of dinner changed, populated by small talk, each unwilling to address what had almost happened between them.

If Eve was being completely honest with herself, she'd wanted the kiss. Wanted to be a part of the emotion, the feeling—something she'd cut herself off from for the last year. She'd needed time to move past the shock of Mark's calling off their engagement out of the blue, and time to process her mother's death.

But how could she explain to herself this crazy desire to jump back in to that feeling, that emotion, with the brother of the man who'd made her cut herself off from it all in the first place?

That would be crazy. And if everything in life happened for a reason and gave opportunities to learn, indulging one more minute of this train of thought would do nothing more than show she hadn't learned the lessons she needed to learn. She needed to play it safe.

And Spencer Canley was not safe.

She knew he was right—he'd just been doing a job both times he'd visited her at the beach house with difficult messages. And she'd heard with her own ears as he'd walked away from it all and quit his job with Mark and his company.

But although she'd heard all those words, only one word actually mattered.

Canley.

Spencer was still a Canley. And she didn't need any more trouble from any more Canleys.

When the water subsided and this particular Canley brother could drive off again, he'd leave, taking the centerpiece of her former engagement ring with him—and hopefully that old set of Mark's clothes. Then all traces of connections to the Canley brothers would be removed from her bungalow and her life.

"Care for a refill?" Spencer held up the carafe of water Eve had placed in the middle of the square butcher block table.

"Just halfway," Eve said, watching as the clear liquid crawled up the smooth curve of the glass.

"Are you okay, Eve?"

She nodded. The truth was she really *was* okay—or she would be as soon as the last vestiges of the Canley family exited her life—but she couldn't go much past that. If she couldn't explain it to herself, how could she explain it to Spencer?

"About earlier—" Spencer started to speak, but Eve waggled her glass in an attempt to cut his train of thought off.

"No, really, Eve, I—" He hesitated again, then picked back up before she could jump in. "I know I should say something like I'm sorry. That's probably the right thing to do. I've been doing the wrong thing by you for too long. I told Mark on the phone you deserved better, and I meant it. So I really should say I'm sorry. But it would be a lie."

Whatever Eve had been expecting, it wasn't that. She stabbed the last bowtie on her plate and tried to buy a little time before answering.

"I'm probably not going to see you again after I leave here, Eve. I won't be running any more errands for Mark." A shadow crossed Spencer's face and he paused, then as he began to speak again, it dissipated. "I told you earlier that you were pretty when you smiled. Eve, you're even pretty with an old towel on your head. You're my brother's ex-fiancée, but you deserve to know that fact. No matter what Mark may have made you think, you're a beautiful woman with a lot to offer."

Warmth plucked at Eve's cheeks from the inside. She lowered her head a bit and hoped Spencer would attribute the blush to the steam coming off the pasta.

"Don't duck your head, Eve. Don't. You should own that truth."

"Spencer, it's not that simple."

"Why not?"

"I've heard it all before, from another Canley brother. He told me everything you just said. Told me it was the truth. Then he left—via a message from a proxy—you. And I've never heard from him again. Worse, I don't know why. I don't know what I did wrong." She choked a little bit on the memories as they traveled from mind to heart and out through her mouth.

"You didn't do anything wrong. It was all Mark. He's been working on this contract for a year and a half, and he wanted it badly. He saw a chance to get in with Moldayev, who had the right connections with the right people to get it done. They met at a cocktail party while you were taking care of your mom. Once he saw where he could go once he got an international partnership established, Mark became obsessed with this contract."

"I remember him talking about it." She'd been in such a fog then, she must have missed the signs that things were going wrong.

"Your mom was dying. But Mark didn't care about that. He didn't care about anything except the next contract that would bring in more money."

"He didn't used to be like that, you know." Eve felt heavy with the memory.

"Don't get up. I've got all of this, remember? My treat. You just sit back and relax." Spencer stood from the table, collected his plate, and then Eve's. "Mark's always been driven, but he didn't used to be obsessed. But like I said, he saw dollar signs, and lots of them, once he realized he had a chance at an international partnership on the scale of Moldayev. It was more fun for David and I when the three Canley brothers were working together on a common goal, doing something we loved. We'd always done things as partners since we were young. But along the way, Mark's only goal became money."

Eve heard the sadness in Spencer's voice and she realized Mark had taken away something very personal from him, too. She wasn't the only one who had been hurt by Mark's single-minded quest to get more and be more.

As an artist, Eve knew the right light could change a picture entirely. She'd already seen Spencer in a bit of a different light this evening. Now, it seemed almost as though one of those lightning strikes outside had brought a bright glow near to them both, changing her perspective.

She'd gone from enmity to empathy.

And it felt like a weight had just dropped from her shoulders.

Her New Year's sabbatical at the beach house wasn't ruined after all. In fact, maybe this was the first of many realizations on the road to finally being free. Maybe this was some kind of sign that she would get the healing she needed, starting now.

"I thought I needed to be alone this weekend to make sense of things and move on," Eve said, more to herself than to him. "Now I think you're here for a reason. I'm not happy about the reason you came, but I'm glad you're here, Spencer."

Spencer loaded the last dish in the small dishwasher. "I'm not glad about the car repair bill that's coming, but I'm glad I'm here, too, Evie."

The rain continued steadily throughout the night. After dinner, Spencer fixed them both a cup of coffee. Eve hung Spencer's wool sweater up to dry and threw his corduroy pants and socks in the dryer with a few towels, so hopefully he'd have suitable clothes to wear when he left in the morning.

When the caffeine had worn off and yawning set in for them both, Eve showed Spencer to the guest bedroom, then went down the short hallway to her own room. The conversation into the early morning hours had stayed steadily casual. No more mentions of Mark, or what could have been in the kitchen. Eve talked about her latest projects and a gallery showing she'd had in Dallas in the fall. Spencer shared stories about his summer vacation, SCUBA diving in the Caribbean. It was more personal than just some general small talk, but still safer than the previous talks of conversation.

It made sense. They weren't strangers. In fact, they'd once been friends. Time had changed so many circumstances, but the heart had a way of never forgetting the good times.

Hearing about Eve's career as an artist fascinated Spencer. Mark had always made it sound like she painted as a hobby, when in reality, Eve was a sought-out painter who exhibited her work around the country. Spencer hadn't ever really thought much about Eve because Mark had never spoken of her in a way which gave Eve her due. But tonight, with the specter of Mark Canley pushed firmly out of the way, all Spencer could do was think about Eve.

Even the sound of the rain and the waves couldn't bring Spencer much fitful rest. He laid awake for hours, watching the clock, the ceiling, the drops sliding down the windowpane. The guest room also served as Eve's studio, and the narrow day bed had been placed in the far corner, giving him a full, moonlit view of Eve's latest project on an easel by the window.

The painting was just beginning to take shape. She'd sketched out the basic form on the canvas and had begun to fill in the first layers of paint. A seagull, flying high against the sun. From his spot in the middle of the bed, Spencer studied the gentle curve of sketched graphite that made up the outlines of what would become a highly complex wing of feathers and light and shadow.

He closed his eyes, turning over the image in his mind. The gull's wing morphed behind his eyelids into something else—a towel falling from softly curled hair darkened several shades by water, illuminated by a lightning strike. He saw Eve's face, saw the shadows on one side and the light on the other. And as he studied the gentle curve of her face and the soft fullness of her lips, he finally fell asleep, using his mind to turn what could have been into the reality of dreams.

Eve loved the quiet of mornings on the beach. The rain had stopped sometime overnight, and the sound of the tide gently roaring was all that broke the stillness. She started a pot of coffee and looked out the window. Today, Spencer would leave, taking the final remnants of her past along with him.

She'd craved that sense of moving on for the past year. But now that it finally seemed here, waiting at her doorstep, she hesitated to open the door. The realization frustrated her. She'd spent a year ridding her mind of thoughts of the Canleys. She'd thought the problem was just thoughts of Mark and what should have been.

Then another Canley walked onto her beach and sent everything haywire. Since when had she cared what Spencer Canley did or what he thought? She wanted to beat her wayward head against the wall—maybe that would banish thoughts of all the Canleys, once and for all.

A rustling sound cut through the roar of the gulf and Eve turned, face to face with the reason for her frustration.

"I guess I'd better go down and check on my car. I looked out the window of the guest room, and it seems like the water has receded."

"It usually does. This whole area is flood prone because of being right at sea level, but once it stops raining, the water usually drains quickly."

Eve poured another cup of coffee in a mug decorated with a scene of beach umbrellas and handed it to Spencer. "How do you like your coffee?"

Spencer reached for the cup, brushing the tops of Eve's fingers where she held the mug as he took the handle. The touch felt light, like the tickle of a cat's whiskers, but the fact that it made her think about the near-miss kiss from last night followed her as close as the constant companionship of a pet dog. It stalked her every move, chased her every thought.

"Oh, I'm pretty simple," Spencer replied, taking a sip.

Eve could barely contain a short laugh of irony. Nothing about Spencer was simple, she'd come to realize.

Certainly not the way her whole range of thoughts had shifted about him from just a few hours of getting to know him better.

Spencer didn't waste time sipping the coffee. He'd finished the whole steaming mug before Eve had enough milk mixed in hers. He walked past her and placed the empty mug in the sink.

"Wish me luck," he said with a wide grin.

"Oh absolutely." Eve buried her head in a long, deep sip of caffeine, wishing luck was all she needed to figure out why watching Spencer walk out the front door left her feeling so hollow. She tried to shift her thoughts back to the coffee, knowing that she didn't want to overthink what had happened in the last day.

Only a few minutes passed before the front door opened again, bringing a brush of early morning air along with Spencer.

"Well, it still won't start. Guess I need to get a mechanic. Know anyone I can call?" Spencer ran a hand through his dark hair.

"Sure. Mike Renwick. He owns a small shop over off 61st Street." Eve picked up her smartphone off the counter and searched for the number. "Want me to call him, or you?"

"Just give me the number. I'll call him." Spencer pulled his own phone out of his back pocket.

"Ok. It's 555-1070."

Spencer dialed with his thumb, then waited as the phone rang. "No answer."

"I know he's around. I just saw him at the grocery store yesterday morning." Eve looked down at the face of her phone and checked the time. She couldn't let Spencer stall around here anymore. She needed to find a way to facilitate his departure off Provident Island. "I'm sure my Jeep is ok, since it sits higher than your car. Why don't we go into town and just go by his shop? He lives in an efficiency on site. I bet we can track him down."

"That sounds perfect. Maybe I can get my car towed over to his place and he can get her running again." Spencer smiled, and Eve couldn't help but notice how white his teeth were.

Which made her thoughts turn inevitably to last night's moment *that wasn't.*

Was everything going to come back to that? What had happened to her? Eve mentally lashed herself. She'd spent years with Mark and never thought about kissing him as much as she'd thought in the last twelve or so hours about *not* kissing Spencer.

She needed to stop, though. Nothing Spencer had done this morning indicated that he still thought about that close call in the kitchen. Everything he'd done and said since walking in the kitchen pointed to one thing—getting his car running and getting out of Port Provident. He probably had plans for tonight.

After all, it was New Year's Eve.

A time to dress up, meet up with someone special, and ring in the New Year. The turn of the calendar. A day made for celebrating possibilities.

Although they'd spent hours talking last night, the truth of the matter remained. Eve didn't really know Spencer. She didn't know if he had someone in his life. They'd carefully avoided any discussion of that. At the time, Eve figured it was because they were trying to avoid talking about Mark, and therefore Eve's former relationship with him.

But there was probably more to it than that.

"I'm ready when you are, Spencer." Eve picked up her keys from the hook on the wall at the edge of the kitchen.

More than that, she was ready to get back to the weekend she planned before the middle Canley brother showed up. She'd had a nice detour last night, settled some old questions in her mind.

But the conversation also opened too many new thoughts in her mind—crazy thoughts, thoughts full of sparks and near-kisses—and it was best if she shut those lines of attraction down before she spent another year trying to get another Canley out of her mind.

"Is something wrong?" Eve responded to a stifled angry word from Spencer as she pulled out on the main highway and pointed the Jeep back toward town.

"Just thinking that I need a car with some off-road capabilities."

"No more sports car, huh?" The traffic was pretty light, and Eve appreciated that. In the summer, this stretch of road was jammed with tourists trying to get from their hotels to the beach and the other attractions Port Provident offered. Driving seemed so much less stressful in the off-season.

Too bad she couldn't put being this close to Spencer in the same category. She'd only had one cup of coffee this morning, but the flashes of adrenaline speeding through her veins made it seem like she'd emptied an entire pot.

"The Jeep definitely seems more conducive for trips to the beach." Spencer watched the waves as they drove back into the city from the beachside neighborhoods.

"Are you planning on making more trips to the beach?" She could only hope her voice sounded calm. Spencer probably had a summer getaway weekend in mind for him and some friends, and nothing more. She could not embarrass herself by reading more into his one line than he could have possibly meant.

"I think I might, yeah." Spencer turned his head toward Eve briefly, then returned to watching the scenery off the edge of Texas. "I can't believe I've never considered spending more time on the island."

Well, so much for trying to not overthink things.

At least she could keep from embarrassing herself, Eve decided, if she kept her stinking mouth shut.

Nothing spoken, nothing to worry about.

Right?

"Do you visit to the beach house often?"

Wrong.

Stay focused, Eve. It's just casual conversation.

"When my mother died, I inherited the beach house. I try to come down and spend one or two weekends a month, but I find myself coming more and more lately. In the spring, I've always liked to paint out on the deck. The light's great and it's nice to spend time in the sun and the breeze. I've been thinking more and more about a way to stay here permanently. But I have relationships with galleries back in Houston. I'm not sure what I'd do here."

Spencer nodded quietly. "So this had been your mom's house?"

"She grew up on the island. This was home for her. And, I guess, in a way, for me too." She put on her blinker and moved to the turn lane. "Lots of memories here."

Some had been good.

Some had been bad.

And some, like last night...well, the jury was still out on how she completely felt about that. She wanted to feel good about it. But the stakes seemed too high. Eve didn't want to look like a fool—not to Spencer—or herself.

"I think I need to make a few more memories here." Spencer smiled as he spoke. Eve caught the grin out of the corner of her eye.

Eve jerked and hit the brake. The Jeep's tires stopped short and the whole car kicked, as though in the wake of a karate chop.

"Eve? You ok?"

So much for not looking like a fool.

Eve scanned the intersection. "Um, I thought I saw something in the street," she muttered, not believing a word of her lame excuse for a second. No doubt Spencer saw through it too.

"Ok. You kind of scared me there."

More muttering. "Sorry."

She made a few turns and brought the Jeep to a stop in the driveway of Renwick Auto Repair. The garage bay was open and a car sat high on the lift.

"That's Mike." Eve pointed to the man standing at the side of the front tire to the gunmetal gray Chevrolet suspended in the air.

"Great. I'll go see if I can talk to him for a second." Spencer opened the door of the Jeep and hopped out, then strode to the edge of the garage bay.

Eve watched as Spencer talked with Mike, turning his hands as he spoke, trying to paint a visual picture of what was happening—or in Spencer's case, not happening—with the car. As she watched the twists and points, Eve's mind flashed back to last night, when those same hands had tangled in the wet twists of her hair and pulled her close.

Too easily, she remembered the jolt of electricity she'd felt.

She'd been held before—she'd been engaged before, so of course she'd been held, been kissed.

But never had those moments caused lightning strikes in her veins that rivaled the real thing cracking just outside.

And never had she spent so much time wondering what could have been after something that could clearly never be.

Because even though she'd heard Spencer give Mark his notice, the fact still remained. Spencer Canley was Eve's former fiancé's brother.

There was no future for Eve in a world with Spencer. That was a world where she'd receive Christmas cards from Mark or see him on holidays or at family events. Her ex had pulled himself out of her life in a selfish, tearing way. He'd left scars on her heart she had only now begun to not feel every time the silence overwhelmed her.

Spending a good deal of her free time in a beach house meant Eve now knew well the sound of silence and the gentle roll of white-noise waves.

If only the man in front of her had been Spencer Smith, or Spencer Jones, or Spencer Black.

Anyone but Spencer *Canley*.

Spencer *Can't*-ley.

As in "You *can't* have a future with your ex-fiancé's brother, Eve."

She wondered how many times she'd have to remind herself of that fact before she finally quit letting her mind wander. Hopefully Mike would get Spencer's car running ASAP so he could go and she could go back to her new year.

Spencer gestured back toward the Jeep. His business-like face broke into a grin as he met Eve's gaze just above the steering wheel. There was no use trying to feign disinterest.

Eve *had* been looking and she just got caught.

"Thanks again," Spencer said to Mike as he opened the door to the Jeep. "You have my number, so just give me a call and let me know. At this point, just make any repair you need to make."

He gave a small jump into the car and slid across the black leather seat. "He's going to take his tow truck out to your place and bring the car back in to check it out. He said he should have a better idea this afternoon."

Eve nodded, but looked straight ahead. If she looked over at him, she knew he'd see right through her—if he hadn't already. "Do we need to head back to the beach house and meet him?"

"Nope. I gave him my keys, and with the car parked under the stilts and not blocked in, he said he could get to it without a problem. Since we didn't have anything but coffee this morning, I thought maybe we could grab a bite to eat. You hungry?"

"Starving, actually."

In fact, she knew she was starving for something she could never have.

But maybe lunch would keep her mind off of things a little longer, until Spencer could cross the Causeway and go back to the mainland.

"How about something with a beach view? Anything good with a view?"

Eve backed out of the lot at Renwick's Auto Repair and headed back toward the main shoreline artery of Port Provident, Gulfview Boulevard. "How about Porter's? They don't have outdoor seating, but they do have lots of windows. And the shrimp bisque is the best I've ever had."

"Sounds perfect. Great view, great food, great company. I think that's exactly what the doctor ordered."

"The doctor?" Eve gave a short laugh. "You mean the mechanic. Mike will love it that you've elevated him to doctor status."

"Well, he did seem like one of the best mechanics I've ever worked with, but no. I was actually talking about a real doctor. Dr. Arthur Mills at the Methodist Hospital of Houston, to be specific."

"Dr. Arthur Mills at the Methodist Hospital of Houston wants you to have a good meal with a view of the beach?" The curiosity got the best of Eve and as she pulled up to the stoplight, she turned and looked at Spencer with full curiosity written across her face.

Spencer looked quietly at the waves for a moment. The light turned green and Eve re-focused back toward the street, then quickly angled into the Porter's parking lot. "Let's go inside. I'll explain more over this bisque you mentioned."

As soon as Eve came to a stop in a parking space, Spencer hopped out of the Jeep. He moved so quickly that he was able to open Eve's door before she'd even tucked her keys in the little pocket at the top of the interior of her purse. It had been a long time since someone had gone out of their way to open a door for her. Even Mark had stopped doing it months before he'd ended their relationship.

If Eve had been one open to conspiracy theories and writing on walls, the slow but sure ebb of "the little things" from Mark should have told her that despite having an engagement ring made from a stone that had belonged to royalty, she wasn't going to get her fairy-tale happily-ever-after.

As they stepped onto the sidewalk and headed toward the door, Spencer brushed his hand lightly and let it rest on the small of Eve's back. Even though it was January, the day was already unseasonably warm at the edge of Texas. The gentle contact of Spencer's palm had the same effect as adding another few degrees to the thermometer.

She glanced briefly down at her watch. Only twelve hours left in this year. Her resolve to start fresh, to quit looking back, to make the coming year one of triumph and new beginnings hadn't changed.

So what would it hurt, she wondered, if she silenced that little voice in the back of her mind for the next seven hundred and twenty minutes?

What if she decided to act like there was no tomorrow?

What if she decided to just forget that Spencer was a Canley and forget that her engagement ring was in his pocket, waiting to go to some other woman?

Everyone made New Year's resolutions, and Eve knew she was no different. Every year since childhood, she would set one key resolution. Her determined spirit would not allow her to break the goals she'd set in front of her.

But for the next twelve hours, Eve Larson decided to make a New Year's Evie resolution. She smiled as she remembered Spencer casually giving her the nickname.

She would give living in the moment her best shot. It would be hard to silence that little skeptic in her head. She resolved to try—no, she resolved to succeed—and enjoy her time with an attractive, intelligent man.

Then, midnight would come and go and she'd turn the page back to her normal, orderly self tomorrow morning.

Chapter Four

S pencer didn't expect the restaurant to be this crowded. But then again, he knew Porter's had reached legendary status on the island generations ago, and a lot of people probably had this final day of the year off from work. Many likely decided to come to the coast and enjoy the winter sunshine that had come out after last night's rain. The mild air and the light splashing off the gentle undulations of the water made the day feel fresh and clean.

He'd been carrying the secret about his upcoming medical treatment for months now, and as he walked behind Eve and the hostess across the wide dining room, Spencer tried to figure out why he'd said anything about Dr. Mills. Couldn't he have explained "just what the doctor ordered" some other way? After all, it was just a phrase. People used it every day and they didn't mean a real doctor. *All those years of boardroom meetings and he couldn't just think up something on the fly?*

Spencer disappointed himself.

But Eve didn't disappoint him at all.

The look on her face when he revealed he was under the care of a doctor at a nationally-recognized hospital radiated true concern. And he knew he'd need to address those concerns as soon as they sat down.

Eve didn't waste any time, scanning the menu briefly, then closing it and laying it off to her left side. "So, you are seeing a doctor? Are you feeling ok?"

Spencer nodded. He could answer that honestly. "I'm feeling better than I have in a long time."

"I don't mean lunch, Spencer." Eve reached out for the slice of crusty warm bread Spencer had cut for her.

"I know you don't. I brought it up, so I guess I have to explain it." He popped a piece of the soft white loaf in his own mouth and used the chewing to stall and gather his thoughts. No going back. "I do have a doctor, a cardiologist to be specific. And he did tell me to go out and do the things I enjoy. To get rid of the stress. That's why I'm not working for Mark anymore."

Eve dusted a few crumbs from her fingers. "You said you weren't working for Mark anymore because he made shady deals."

"He's not doing anything illegal. He's just always played in a gray area, and I've finally decided I've had enough. I've tried to help him see the light for years, and I've finally realized he's the leopard that won't change his spots. His lack of business ethics—or at least that's how I see it—was causing too much stress in my life. And that began affecting my health. Last year, about the time I last saw you, I'd been getting dizzy and finding myself short of breath. I explained it away every possible way, but nothing I did made things any better. Finally, I went in to a doctor to find out what was wrong. After a bunch of tests, he referred over to Dr. Mills, who discovered not too long ago that I have a patch of cardiac tissue that gets off rhythm."

"That sounds serious."

"It's become that way, actually. Initially, we tried treating it with medication. But it looks like I'm going to have surgery later in January."

"Can they fix it?" Eve leaned toward Spencer in a subconscious non-verbal expression of concern.

"Yes, he said they can. It's called an ablation. They go in with a laser and destroy those cells that are causing arrhythmia." Spencer pulled off another chunk of bread. "So for me, ultimately, there's good news."

Eve's gaze bored down on Spencer. He could feel her searching him, almost like a pat-down at the airport. The idea of Eve's hands touching him again like last night, light as snow, made his mind wander far from technical details of impending heart surgery.

"So why do you have this panicked look on your face?"

"I do?" He certainly wouldn't classify himself as panicked—although it wouldn't be a stretch to say his blood pressure was elevated.

Except that had nothing to do with the heart condition.

"You do." Eve's face was shadowed with concern. "I know we're not close friends and we've got kind of a strange history, but Spencer, if you need someone to talk to, I'd be happy to listen. We used to be friends. I think we could still be friends. It seems like you've got a lot going on right now with quitting your job and going in for surgery."

"I guess so. I hadn't thought about it that way. I'm more of a one-thing-at-a-time guy." He buttered the rest of his bread slice as he collected his thoughts. "I guess I'm a compartmentalist."

The waiter came and took their order. Spencer followed Eve's assurances that he wouldn't be sorry with an order of both a cup of Porter's famous shrimp bisque and by topping his starter salad with the house-made honey-pecan vinaigrette. "That dressing sounds a little girly, Eve."

She laughed a little as she handed her menu to the waiter. "You don't like things that are sweet?"

Spencer didn't look away and didn't stop the words that popped into his mind from coming out. "I like you."

He raised one eyebrow, but quickly changed his expression. He didn't want to look like a cartoon character.

A light flush prickled Eve's cheeks. Spencer knew he'd caught her off-guard.

He wasn't exactly sure if he meant to or not. And he wasn't sure where to go from here. "Does that bother you?"

"No," she said after a thoughtful pause. "I guess not. I mean, I don't know."

"You don't know?" Spencer's inner negotiating strategist kicked in. Maybe if he could get to the core of Eve's thoughts, he could figure out his own.

The waiter brought two white cups filled to the brim with a thick orange cream soup. The steam tickled Spencer's nose with a scent that confirmed all of Eve's endorsements.

"You just said you were a compartmentalist," Eve said.

She blew on the first hot spoonful, and Spencer flashed back quickly to last night. He brought that train to a screeching halt. They were having a good, comfortable conversation. He wasn't about to let anything derail that.

He nodded, encouraging her to continue before he said anything further.

"I think I'm a big-pictureist. Well, I am, if that's a word." She laughed a little, the high pitched sound bringing the small curve of a smile to her lips and to Spencer's own. "As an artist, I look at the big picture, you know? I see the play of light, the small details, the sensory interplay in a moment. Then I try to bring it all together and capture it."

"So, what do you see here?" Spencer decided to draw her out even further. He wanted to hear more of what she had to say.

The hesitancy on Eve's face stood out as plainly as the smattering of sun-kissed freckles that dusted her nose. "What do you mean?"

"What's the big picture? What do you see here?"

"You. I see you." She leaned over the cup of bisque, neatly shading her eyes from Spencer's view.

He'd been in many board rooms and found a way to cut many deals. But Eve could have held her own in any of them. She was playing her cards close to the vest—while giving him just enough to keep him thinking about her next move. He'd started them down this rabbit trail. He would keep the conversation going and see where it led.

"Anything else?"

"Soup. Bread." She turned her head toward the window. "The ocean."

Spencer didn't know whether he should laugh at her stalling or be irritated by it. He decided the former would probably get his experiment the results he was hoping for. "Anything else?"

"What's with the twenty questions, Spencer?"

The waiter came and refilled their glasses of tea and brought another loaf of bread nestled in a dark blue napkin.

"Did it bother you that I said I liked you?" May as well cut to the chase, rather than risking a snuffing out of all the goodwill that seemed to have been generated since last night's clearing of the air.

Spencer wished she'd look up so he could gauge her reaction. Instead, she kept her head gently bowed and ate another spoonful of the velvety appetizer before answering.

"I guess not." Her reply seemed as unsteady as a newcomer to a tightrope act.

"That doesn't sound too convincing to me." He scraped the spoon around the bottom curve of the cup and collected the last bit of his bisque for a final bite. "You were right, you know."

"I was?" Eve finally looked up. Her eyes glowed like a rich golden topaz stone. He'd seen that light before. And this time, he didn't want to close off the memory.

"You were. About a couple of things, actually. One, this bisque is fantastic. Thanks for the recommendation." Spencer pushed the now-empty cup and saucer to the corner of the table. "And you were right that we have something of a strange history."

"But?" She accurately picked up that he was holding something back. Maybe there was a little bit of deal-maker in her artist's heart after all.

"But I think I'd like it if that wasn't always the case."

He knew full well—heck, he expected it—that she could reject this offer of friendship. They could eat their meal in a general, awkward silence, then pick up his car and part ways forever. She'd be through with the Canley brothers.

But, Spencer wondered, now that they'd said things that had been left unsaid for a year or more, now that he'd heard her laugh and he'd seen a small sliver of her hopes and dreams—now that he'd come so close to kissing her and couldn't stop himself from wanting more—would this Canley brother ever be through with her?

He shook his head and took a deep breath.

And then he waited for Eve's reply.

"I don't know, Spencer."

Spencer felt the adrenaline in his veins slam on the brakes and do a quick retreat, leaving with a whoosh. It felt like someone was standing on his chest.

He knew it was his heart.

And just as surely, he knew it wasn't something surgery could fix.

Eve pushed her empty white ramekin to the side, and then met Spencer's gaze with studious purpose.

"But I made you an offer, and I intend to keep that. You need a friend. And what kind of person would I be if I based whether or not I could be your friend on the actions of someone who isn't sitting here at this table?" She tucked a stray lock of hair behind her ear. "Mark didn't think I was good enough to keep around. He needed a newer, flashier model. I wouldn't want to think you judged me on the basis of Mark's actions. And I won't judge you based on them, either."

She made total sense. "I understand your hesitation, Eve."

Eve raised her fingers off the table, in a shy gesture designed to stop him from speaking further. "I don't want to be a compartmentalist, Spencer. I thought I wanted to pack the last year or so of my life in a box and never deal with it again. I thought I wanted tonight to be that line in the sand for me, when I declared I was officially not looking back. I wanted a new year with a new beginning. The thought of it is the only thing that's kept me sane these last few months. I've been just hanging on, waiting to experience this night, this New Year's Eve, this moment...and fully embrace what it meant to me."

She hesitated, but Spencer knew this wasn't the right time for him to jump into her train of thought. He held back from speaking.

"Now, though, I think if I do what I thought I was supposed to do...I'm going to cut myself off from a part of Eve Larson. The experiences of the last year, good and bad, have helped make me who I am. I'm stronger, I know how much I can take. I don't want to walk away from that. If I want to see the big picture like I say I do, then I can't cut myself off. I have to see the good with the bad and make something beautiful from them both."

The waiter appeared with two plates loaded with fresh gulf shrimp prepared three different ways, atop a bed of rice pilaf. Eve kept talking as the plate was slid in front of her.

"I guess what I'm trying to say is that I'm glad we were able to talk last night and clear up some things, Spencer. And I think I'm ok with not closing that off in the past. I meant what I said, we have a strange history, but it doesn't necessarily have to repeat itself in the future."

The jingle from his cell phone interrupted Spencer before he could agree with her proposal. "It's Mike from the garage. Do you mind if I take this?"

"No, not at all. Go ahead." Eve squeezed a lemon wedge over the grilled shrimp at the edge of her plate.

The gravelly-voiced mechanic cut right to the chase. He had the little sports car in his possession and was working on it, but he'd need a few more hours to get everything taken care of.

"That's fine, Mike. Take your time. I appreciate you fitting me in on short notice." Spencer wanted to wrap up the call both so Mike could get back to work on the car without any further delay...and because Spencer wanted to turn his full attention back to Eve.

He'd come to the island to do a job, to take back a piece of jewelry that meant two very different things to two very different people.

And although he had spent his entire life around one of those people, the one who intrigued him most was the woman he'd only just begun getting to know.

Spencer wanted to talk with her more. He wanted to see some of that big picture she spoke of.

He already knew one thing for sure. The biggest mistake of his brother's life wasn't going to be losing some telecom deal in some far off land. It was going to be pushing away this soul-searching woman with the honey-topaz eyes and the incredible ability to adjust to life's blows and keep moving forward.

Spencer had plenty of regrets from following Mark's lead too many times during the years when they worked together.

He speared a bite of shrimp with more force than was probably necessary as he resolved to not create a Mark-inspired regret in his personal life too.

Eve had spoken several times of her desire to make today, New Year's Eve, a day that counted in her life, one she'd remember as a day she took back control of her life from the grief she'd endured the past year or so.

Many people planned their resolutions weeks or months ahead for the year to come. Spencer usually ignored the custom altogether. He prided himself on being make-a-decision-on-the-spot kind of guy. He'd always thought making resolutions indicated you were failing in an area and needed to make some kind of full overhaul. And he was not a man who dealt in failure.

But this New Year's Eve, Spencer decided to make a resolution.

He resolved to get to know Eve Larson better.

"Do you have any plans for this afternoon, Eve?" Spencer hoped his voice sounded casual.

She ate the last bite of rice from the middle of her plate, then shook her head. "I don't think so. Why?"

"Well, it looks like it's going to be a few more hours until Mike gets my car fixed." He laid his silverware on the edge of his plate and signaled the waiter to bring their check. "Isn't the Port Provident downtown area supposed to be something special?"

"Yes, it's on the National Register of Historic Places. Most of the buildings are more than a hundred years old. Lots of buildings that survived the Great Storm of 1910."

"The big hurricane?" Spencer vaguely remembered a story about a giant hurricane at the turn of the last century which overwhelmed Port Provident.

"Right. One of the largest natural disasters in American history. Thousands upon thousands of lives lost—not to mention countless homes and dreams. The island is dotted with beautiful old buildings that survived and there are lots of great shops downtown in many of those old buildings and even some neat attractions like a movie about the Great Storm."

He didn't do a whole lot of shopping as a rule, but maybe there would be a trinket down there that Eve liked. He would love to see her eyes take on that topaz sparkle again.

Quickly, Spencer made resolution two: Make Eve's eyes light up. This could be a fun conclusion to a conflict-filled year.

"That actually sounds interesting. Maybe a history lesson is a good way to close out the last twelve months." He signed the receipt for lunch and waved off Eve's attempt to put cash for her portion of the meal in the padded black folder. "This is my treat. You've helped me fix my car and gave me a place to stay last night. Are you ready to go explore downtown?"

Eve stood up from the table and a shy smile tugged at the corners of her cotton-candy lips. The simple change lightened her entire face. She looked soft, sweet, and completely desirable.

Resolution three: Kiss Eve...before they rang in the new year.

Chapter Five

The closest parking spot Eve could find was a few blocks to the north of the downtown lot she generally preferred to park in.

"There must be something going on today. It's usually only this crowded for Santas on the Street, or Mardi Gras, or festivals like that." Eve could feel warmth coming off Spencer that cut through the salt-tinged end-of-December chill.

She stood a little more than a ruler's length away from Spencer Canley, and it was impossible to deny his presence.

She definitely wasn't alone now.

What surprised her the most, though, was she didn't want to change a thing.

Perhaps plans were made to be broken.

The air was crisp, yet pleasant—a perfect Texas December day. Looking up, Eve could see the sun perched at the top of the sky. It shone brightly, golden as a canary. It felt good to be a part of a crowd that milled around, savoring the last few hours of the year.

And if Eve leveled with herself more than she was usually comfortable leveling, it felt good to share those last few hours of the year with a handsome man who just flashed a confident smile in her direction.

Just that one look lifted her feet a few inches off the ground and lifted her spirits more than she'd thought possible when she'd crossed the causeway the day before to begin her time of reflection.

What on earth was happening to her?

"Do you make it down here for many of those tourist festivals?"

They stopped at the corner to let cars pass before they entered the crosswalk.

"No, not really. I don't make it to the Island as much as I'd like, period. I told you earlier that I want to be a full-time resident here, truthfully, but I haven't figured out how to make that work. I have a part-ownership interest in a small gallery in Houston, and most of the galleries that I display in are there too. So, that keeps me over on the mainland most of the time. And then when I am here, I'm usually trying to paint. I generally have a set amount of time to get work done. I don't typically come down here to relax or vacation. I come here to create and dream."

Spencer nodded. "This seems like a good place to do that. There's something about seeing waves and taking sea breezes into your lungs that speaks to one's soul."

"So, you get it, too." Eve found herself looking at her feet. Then her steps stilled. "Lately, all my dreams have been about endings and the past. I don't want to do that anymore. I want a way that I can be here—live here, work here, create here. I'd love to be a Provident Islander, but I just don't know how. I'm an artist. I'm not really a businessperson. I do some things at the gallery, but Kit runs the show. I'm window dressing."

"I know someone who knows a thing or two about business, you know. All you have to do is ask." Spencer looked up at the small orange building with the green shutters they'd halted in front of. "The Island Jewelry Box. Looks cute. Do you want to start our tour of downtown shopping here?"

Eve squinted one eye and raised an eyebrow.

"What?" Spencer matched her skeptical look with one of his own.

"You're a guy. First, you asked to come to a tourist shopping district. And now you want to go in a jewelry store?"

"Are you questioning my man card?"

Eve adjusted her gaze and took in the full picture that was Spencer Canley. He was back in the same corduroy pants and lightweight green wool sweater—dry after Eve's ministrations on their behalf yesterday. Eve knew she might have been poking fun at him, but there was one thing she definitely was *not* doing. And that was questioning anything about Spencer's man card. He was all man. She'd be lying if she even tried to deny that to herself, or to anyone.

"No, of course not," she said crisply. Even if she couldn't convince herself otherwise, he didn't need to know she'd been thinking like that. He'd think she was crazy. She was his brother's ex-fiancée, for crying out loud.

But then again, there'd been that moment in the kitchen last evening. It had probably been clear on her face that she'd been thinking wild thoughts in that moment. How she'd managed to keep her arms at her side and not pull Spencer closer, she still didn't know.

Maybe miracles could still happen.

"Well, then, let's go in." Spencer took a small step to the side, allowing Eve to enter first through the forest green-painted door.

Eve held very few expectations for such a tiny little shop. It seemed like some builder a century ago decided to fill in a tiny space with a shoebox between two larger, multi-story buildings. The structures on either side probably once held bounties like a mercantile for the town's citizens or a cotton exchange for the merchants who had previously relied on the bustling deep water port of Port Provident to trade their wares around the world. By contrast, this little shop didn't even look large enough to have once served as a horse's stable. But it had a 1910 Storm Survivor plaque on it, so Eve knew that though it looked small, these four walls had stood the test of time.

"Welcome to The Island Jewelry Box." A petite woman with trendy hair styled in choppy layers stood behind the counter, wearing a few of the store's pieces. Eve looked around. Glass cabinets and shelves lined the walls. Far from her misgivings when she stood outside, Eve realized this little space had been perfectly outfitted. It was indeed a life-sized jewelry box.

"Thank you," Spencer said as he walked in and closed the door behind him. "You've got a lot more in here than I thought you'd have."

The lady behind the counter smiled. "The best things come in small packages."

As Eve slowly made her way down the display case, she thought of that oft-said phrase in a new light. Maybe the last twenty-four hours qualified. Maybe the best times were going to fit in the last few hours of the three hundred and sixty five days of this long year.

"What is this?" Eve leaned over a dramatic necklace on a display tucked in the back right hand corner of the glass cabinet. It was big, it was bold, and it appealed to the artist's soul inside Eve.

It excited the muse within that had been dormant for so, so many months.

The woman slid the mirrored back door open, pulled out the necklace, and laid it on a black velvet rectangle in front of Eve. "It's turquoise, obviously, interlaced with spiny oyster." She fingered a narrow sliver of orange tucked between chunks of turquoise rock.

Eve reached for the necklace.

"Go ahead, try it on." The sales lady scooted a mirror closer to Eve and then held the necklace out toward her.

Eve had no intention of buying the necklace. It had to cost a fortune. She could see the craftsmanship and detail and knew such workmanship didn't come at a cheap price.

But the voice in her soul whispered...*go ahead...don't hold back...there's no harm in trying*. She'd made a resolution to herself only an hour ago—and she wanted to practice keeping it. She wasn't going to end the year wondering what might have been—about anything.

Instinctively, her hand reached out and touched the top strand of the necklace. The turquoise felt smooth, solid, and a little cool to her fingertips.

"Eve, go ahead." The sound of Spencer's voice mixed with the insistent whisper in Eve's soul. "You really should."

She took hold of the necklace, unfastened the clasp, and laid the ends over her shoulder.

A feather light touch flicked underneath her hair and Eve's breath caught in her throat at the repeat of last night's stolen moment when Spencer's fingers threaded through the wet curls that fell at her neck.

Spencer opened the clasp at the end of the necklace, then fastened it. It seemed like time stood still. She'd never had it take so long to fasten a piece of jewelry, but yet, she didn't want it to end. She didn't want Spencer to take his hands away and take a step back.

The necklace may have been out of her price range, but being here with Spencer seemed somehow priceless...

Once again, his touch made her wish he was just Spencer and she was just Eve and they could enjoy each other's company without all the ghosts of other people and past actions dogging every step.

But just for today, just for the duration of her last-minute resolution—she would pretend that's all they were.

"Do you like it?" Spencer reached around Eve and lifted the heavy oak-framed mirror so she could get a better look. With his other hand, he lifted her hair free of the dramatic beadwork so she could better judge the effect.

Eve turned her head slightly to the right. "It's gorgeous."

"So are you."

If Spencer hadn't been standing so close to Eve, she might have missed his low tones. But she didn't. And she couldn't quite decide how she felt about it.

She wanted to accept it at face value, that a handsome man whose company she was coming to enjoy paid her a high compliment. That would fit in with the new resolution. But those echoes of the past—of engagements broken and letters of demand and a diamond tucked in an envelope—spoke up and rattled in her mind. She fought desperately to push them back into silence.

Eve turned her head a little more and looked Spencer straight in the eye.

"Take the compliment, Evie. Don't overthink it." He didn't back down from her stare. "And don't deny it."

How was she supposed to answer that?

Before she came up with some answer that would likely fall short of what she *needed* to say and surely fall short of what she *wanted* to say, the woman behind the counter cut into the moment.

"So, what do you think?" The woman behind the counter smiled as she inquired.

Think? She couldn't think. Not with Spencer's hands still tangled in her hair and his presence woven into her life. But she owed the pleasant lady some kind of answer.

"I think it's inspiring. It's so unique."

"Everything in this store is handmade by a local artist. Nothing in here is mass-produced. Nothing is from outside of Provident County. That piece is one-of-a kind." She smiled as Eve turned back to the mirror and studied her reflection further.

Spencer let Eve's hair fall back on her shoulders, over the top of the turquoise and burnished shell, then he placed the mirror back on the glass countertop. "Eve's an artist too."

"Really? What kind?"

The tactical question brought her back to reality with a jolt. "Watercolor mostly. Some oil."

"How wonderful. Do you show in one of the galleries here on the island?"

Eve shook her head. "I'm the co-owner of a small gallery in the Houston Heights. But I've been coming to Port Provident since I was a child and many of my paintings are scenes from down here. I would love to find the right place to show a few of my pieces."

"You should talk to Stella next door. She's always looking for new local artists to show in her gallery. She's actually getting close to retirement and is looking for someone to buy the gallery from her, if you know anyone in your artist circles who might be interested. It's a great location."

Eve knew this was the point where she should take the necklace off and hand it back to the sales person. Yet, she hesitated, unsure if her reluctance was because of the attachment she felt to the dramatic creation around her neck or because she hoped for one last touch from Spencer.

"I'll ask around. It sounds like a very good opportunity." She paused, gathered a breath, and then pressed on with the sentence that would end the moment that felt more like a dream than reality. "I guess I should give this back to you."

She lifted her hands to the clasp, but Spencer's fingers were already there. His fingertips landed light as feathers on her neck and deftly worked the clasp open. Eve took a deep breath, trying to drink in the last few seconds of the connection.

"You don't have to, you know." The sales lady's smile grew as she looked from Eve, to Spencer, then back to Eve. "Right, sir?"

Spencer held the necklace in place, and Eve's inhales remained long and slow. "She's right, Evie."

Once again, Eve reached her hands back, and this time laid her hands over Spencer's, plucking the ends of the strands of turquoise from his fingers.

Suddenly, she heard her mother's voice in a memory from years ago. *"You can't always have everything you want, Eve. No matter how wonderful something is, or how much we'd like to have it, sometimes we just can't."*

Her mother had given the wisdom to her only child, and she was still right even when the girl was no an adult. She couldn't have the expensive necklace. And she couldn't have Spencer.

And no pie-in-the-sky lofty resolution about living in the moment would change that. Because after this year ended, reality would still be all around.

Her magical resolution would end at midnight on New Year's Eve. Once the fireworks ceased their popping and their magic, her resolution to leap without looking, to feel without thinking would have to come to an end as well. Reality would be her companion once again instead of Spencer.

"No, really. I can't."

"Well, just think about it. If you change your mind, it'll be here waiting on you." The brunette draped the necklace back over the display and slid it back to the open spot in the cabinet. "Everyone who comes in here tries it on. But really, it looked stunning on you. You have the long neck and the right shoulders to carry it off. I'd love to have it, but I'm too petite. It overwhelms me. But on you..."

"It was perfect." Spencer's voice rang with authority.

Eve gave the necklace in the case one last, wistful look. "Thank you. You have a wonderful shop."

"You're welcome. Thank you for coming in. And definitely go talk with Stella. If you have some Port Provident-inspired pieces, I know she'd love to see them." She turned to acknowledge another couple who walked in the shop and immediately gravitated to the dramatic teal and orange necklace in the corner of the mirror and glass display.

Once they stepped on the sidewalk, Spencer's phone rang. He pulled it out of his pocket and answered without even looking at the screen. "Spencer Canley."

Eve couldn't hear anything the person on the other side of the phone said, but clearly Spencer did not appreciate the message.

"No, I'm still here on the island. I told you I wasn't going to be back on the mainland in time for your arbitrary deadline."

Mark.

Eve felt the muscle at the base of her jaw tighten. The locking made her bottom molars grind into their top counterparts.

She hadn't talked to Mark since two days before he sent Spencer to inform her that he'd decided to end their engagement. From the tone of voice, it seemed clear that she and Spencer shared similar feelings on talking with one particular Canley brother.

"No, we're downtown. Yes, I have it with me. We're just waiting for my car to get repaired." Spencer paused, and then shot back with the rapid staccato of a machine gun. "None of your business, Mark."

He pulled the phone away from his ear and tapped the glass of the screen decisively.

Eve decided her best reaction came down to simple silence. It felt strange to know Mark had been on the other end of the line. And while there'd been a time when she had plenty of words to say to Mark, a peace came over her and she realized that now, she couldn't think of a single thing she cared to waste her breath on saying to him.

She'd spent a year feeling sorry for herself, thinking of everything she'd lost. And while yes, she'd always mourn the absence of her mother, perhaps when it came to the marriage that wasn't, maybe she'd been looking at it all wrong.

Maybe she hadn't lost.

Maybe she'd found.

She'd found she was stronger than she'd ever known possible.

She'd found that she hadn't lost her muse, that she was still capable of being an artist and creating and dreaming.

She'd found that the man she thought she knew and loved was a mirage driven by power and money, two things she didn't much care about.

And, as she was coming to realize, maybe most surprisingly, she'd found a friend in Spencer Canley.

He placed his hand lightly at the small of her back and her burden lightened a little more as her heart quickened with a double-time flutter.

Her spirit lightened, like the lingering glow after a gentle kiss. They began to walk down the sidewalk again, each lost in their own set of thoughts.

Maybe she'd found something she never knew she needed.

Of course Mark would call. He just couldn't leave well enough alone. He couldn't stand not calling the shots. Well, he would need to get used to it. They were brothers, but the term didn't have much of the traditional meaning of bonding when it came to them. Not anymore. Spencer tried to pinpoint when everything started going wrong between them, but he really couldn't.

He did know it had begun longer ago than he'd ever acknowledged—until now. One gray decision after another. One more step that was neither black nor white.

One more lie to his conscience. He wasn't doing it anymore. The decision not only lightened his mind but lightened his heart as well. He'd done the right thing for himself by walking away from working for Mark.

But he wasn't finished. He'd come to Port Provident to reclaim the engagement ring Mark gave to Eve—or as Eve put it, to hide "behind fancy legal words in long documents."

He'd been a bully. And he could tell himself that it was what his boss told him to do, and that everything in there was perfectly, accurately legal.

But the ability to hold up in a court of law didn't change the disgust he felt in his heart as he thought about it. His stomach turned and he wished the jewelry store had sold colorful antacid tablets alongside the bracelets and baubles. He'd have bought them out of stock, just for the chance to try and get rid of the sick feeling inside.

"Do you want to go in the gallery, Eve?" He could barely talk due to the sour blast in his throat. "Isn't this the place the jewelry clerk was talking about?"

Eve leaned forward to peer around Spencer and into the windows of the building. "Looks like it. Sure, let's go in. I'd like to see some of the work being done by local painters."

Spencer reached behind her to open the door.

"Spencer! Stop!" The voice rang out loudly from the small parking lot across the street.

The realization made Spencer's head turn farther to the side than he'd ever thought possible. He didn't need to crane his neck, though. He'd heard that voice his whole life.

"Eve, why don't you go inside?" Spencer tried to keep his voice even.

She grabbed Spencer's hand and threaded her fingers between his own. It felt completely unexpected and completely perfect, but he didn't have time to process his thoughts about it.

"What is Mark doing here?"

"Impatient jerk. He said on the phone he was headed down here. I didn't think he was actually on the island. He's coming for your ring. He needs to get it to the jeweler so he can get it reset before a big dinner at the Consulate next week. All of Moldayev's oligarch friends will be there. It's a big deal. Mark can't just propose to Svetlana Moldayeva. He has to make a big show of it. She wants the headlines and he wants her daddy's approval."

Reflexively, Spencer put his other hand deep in his pocket where the small envelope with Eve's diamond still securely rested.

He didn't think of it as Mark's diamond, even though Mark clearly did. In fact, he couldn't think about anything but Eve. She hadn't seen Mark in well over a year. Mark hadn't even been face to face with her to end their engagement—he'd ordered Spencer to dirty his hands with that task. What was Eve going to think? What was she going to say?

Would she be able to speak at all?

Spencer would not be a bully this time. He would be a protector. He would not let Mark hurt Eve any more. Not when she was so close to putting the defeats of the past behind her. She'd set goals for herself, and as her friend, Spencer would support her in them, no matter the consequences. There was no gray here—only black and white—and Spencer knew exactly where he stood.

Spencer tightened his grip on her fingers with a little squeeze. He wanted to protect her, to keep her from having to live through the next few minutes.

But he couldn't. It was all happening too fast. Mark was already out of the car and about to cross the street.

"Spencer, I said stop."

"Mark, you can't just order me around like a dog."

Mark stepped onto the sidewalk, just feet from where Spencer and Eve stood. Eve took a small step back, so she lined up just barely behind Spencer's shoulder. Spencer recognized it as an unconscious move of self-protection.

"You're not a dog. Dogs are loyal. You're worse." Mark locked his gaze on Eve. "At least no one would be surprised by a dog coming behind and picking up the scraps. Just give me the ring, Spencer."

He held out his hand.

Spencer shifted to the left and blocked Eve from her past just a little more.

"No."

"What?" Mark's nostrils flared with ill-concealed rage.

"I said no, Mark."

Mark swore at his brother, a blue streak of words blasting into the space between them. The ice in his voice cut through the warm December day.

Spencer's left hand held Eve's. His right held the three carats in question. And his future held the big unknown, because once he said what he was about to say, Mark would be on the phone to anyone who would listen, trashing Spencer's reputation to shreds and ruining any good chance he had to find a new job anytime within his circle of business contacts.

"In the state of Texas, an engagement ring is considered a conditional gift, with fault considerations. You are not entitled to getting the ring back because although the wedding never occurred—the condition of the gift—you are the one who ended the engagement. Your whole life, you've been babied and built up, and there haven't been many consequences for your actions. But that ends now. You're at fault, Mark. How you got your lawyer to write this for you, I don't know. But the one thing I do know is I'm no longer going to be a party to bullying Eve for something that has meaning to her and that she has a right to keep."

Mark started to spit more epithets at Spencer. Spencer kept his voice even and only raised it just loud enough to be heard over the racket his spoiled, power-drunk brother was making.

"I can't defend you or make excuses for you anymore. The best thing I ever did was quit working for you. Get in your car and go back home, Mark, and go buy your tabloid fiancée some other expensive rock to demonstrate your abiding love."

Spencer took two steps forward and began to walk toward the door of the gallery. Eve didn't follow him. Instead, she stood as still as the Victorian-style light pole nearby.

"I spent a lot of time this year hating you, Mark Canley. I spent days—months, really—thinking of how you'd ripped away the future I thought I had. And I didn't have anyone around who cared how much it hurt. My mother was gone and I didn't know how I was going to rebuild my life."

Mark turned and began to walk off, like the spoiled child he had always been.

Eve refused to back down. Spencer recognized the courage she was letting flow from inside her heart, putting that gift of truth and compassion out to the world. It had taken him a long time to gather the courage to stand up to Mark too.

"You can walk away from me, Mark Canley, but you can't walk away from who you are. I thought I'd lost everything. Turns out I found myself."

She stood strong on the sidewalk. Mark never looked back. He put his phone to his ear, presumably calling some attorney, Spencer figured. The next sound was tires squealing as he turned his car viciously onto Harborview Drive as fast as he could, headed back to the mainland and the shallow anger that framed his entire life.

"Come on, let's go inside. We're supposed to be looking at pretty things like art, remember?" Spencer could barely hear Eve's voice as she stepped past him.

Spencer held tight to her hand and tugged. "Wait just a second."

Eve turned around, so close Spencer could smell her perfume. It smelled deep and floral. Just like her—beautiful, but with a well-defined edge you couldn't miss if you took the time to get to know her.

"What?" Her eyes glowed like a cat's. The honey tones stood out from the darker brown flecks, all light and glitter. Her face remained blank, like a canvas that had yet to be transformed into a masterpiece. He still held her hand tightly and couldn't tell if the slow, steady heartbeat he felt under his thumb was hers or his own.

He pulled the envelope out of his other pocket and handed it to her. "This belongs to you."

She took it and looked at it, all emotion masked behind a blank stare.

Eve took two steps forward and closed the space between them. The mask fell from her eyes and Spencer read her clearly.

Using his free hand, he threaded his fingers back into her hair, just as he had the night before. But now, he had no intention of letting go or moving back. Instead, he adjusted the palm of his hand and she followed his lead, angling her head gently upward.

He didn't close his eyes. He wanted to take in everything about the moment as it happened. He knew he'd remember these slow-turning seconds for the rest of his life. The gentle curl of Eve's hair and the way it laid softly, like a cat's whiskers, between his fingers. The ivory of her skin, flushed with a light pink from the slight crisp in the Texas December air. The fire that lit her eyes with shades of leaves and autumn as he drew closer. And the feel of silk as he pressed their lips together.

He'd seen plenty of fireworks displays on New Year's Eve, but never before had Spencer felt the crackle and fire in his blood like this.

Eve reached her arm around and pressed the back of Spencer's neck. He felt the corner of the envelope tease a path through the edge of his hairline. The unexpected rasp sent a pop from the base of his skull down to his toes. Spencer lost himself as he became aware of the pressure of Eve's arm, keeping them close.

He didn't want to come out of the moment, and decided he wouldn't until she first moved. Slowly, she dragged her arm back around the curve of his neck and down the plane of his shoulder. As her hand crossed his chest, Spencer felt his breath escape slowly.

"I think I found something that belongs to both of us," Eve said in a soft voice, her hand resting over the spot on his chest where his heart couldn't slow down.

Spencer adjusted his grip on her hand, where they'd stayed connected—through Mark's outburst, through the kiss, and hopefully through much more. "You did."

He guided her through the narrow double doors, filled with a clarity he hadn't known before. The future remained undefined for now, but if he kept Eve in his life—kept her kisses for himself—he knew he'd have more than most.

"Welcome to Stella's at the Shore." A high-pitched voice greeted them as soon as they walked through the door. "Happy New Year."

"It is indeed," Spencer said.

Eve looked up at him and smiled. She didn't say a word, but she didn't need to. Spencer knew. Tonight wouldn't signal the end of things. In just a few hours, they would ring in a beginning together.

They walked toward the back, where an exposed red brick wall had been transformed into a dramatic display for a series of black and white photographs. The unique angles the photographer used revealed well-concealed secrets hidden in facades of historic buildings around Port Provident. It was as though Spencer saw houses and storefronts for the first time.

He looked at Eve, standing a few feet back from the photos. She studied the display with a practiced eye. The photos had caught Spencer's eye, but not like the beautiful woman in front of them. As she took in the framed works on the wall, Spencer took in her.

He'd come down to Port Provident to take something away.

But instead, he felt like he'd been given so much more.

Without his regular job to go back to, this would be a new year with a new start for him. He could only hope that it also held a new relationship with this woman he'd been aware of for years, but never truly knew until now.

His phone vibrated in his pocket. Spencer carefully pulled it out and checked the name before answering. He wasn't about to have any more words with his brother today. Thankfully, the number was a local Port Provident number, which meant it was probably Mike at the garage.

He tapped Eve on the shoulder. "It's Mike. I need to get this."

She nodded with a smile.

"Spencer Canley."

"Spencer, this is Mike. I have an update on your car. Unfortunately, it looks like the last part I need to finish your car isn't in stock here in my garage and my supplier is already closed for New Year's. I'm not going to be able to finish the car today, and they're closed tomorrow too. It'll be the morning of the second before I can wrap this up."

Eve had moved to a group of paintings in the corner. The light from the nearby window fell on her hair and teased a glow in the strands and waves. Spencer followed her with his eyes as he talked to the mechanic.

"You know, Mike, that's ok." A smile came to Spencer's face as he watched Eve's love for the art around her. "I think I'm going to be staying for a while."

Spencer ended the conversation and walked back to Eve.

"How's your car? Is it ready yet?"

He shook his head, but couldn't shake his smile. "No, he's missing a part. It'll be a couple of days since everything is closed for New Year's."

"My guest room is always open." Eve matched Spencer's smile with one of her own. "And I hear there are some pretty amazing fireworks happening on the beach tonight."

"You know, I hear that too." Spencer leaned down and boldly brought his lips back to Eve's, re-igniting that spark they'd found on the sidewalk minutes before. "In fact, I hear they've already gotten started."

Chapter Six

"I'm a traffic accident waiting to happen," Eve said, as she handed Spencer the keys to her Jeep and asked him to drive back to the beach house. The light was fading in the sky, but the ideas in her head were burning brightly.

"Ok, tell me what you're thinking," Spencer asked once they got in the car and began to roll down the stretch of highway along the coast.

"I'm thinking about Stella's. I loved everything about the gallery. It's almost exactly what I've been dreaming about for years. But I've always held back."

She broke from the trance-like gaze out the window she'd had since they got in the car and turned to look at Spencer. His hair blew in the coastal wind and he held the steering wheel with one hand while he balanced his elbow on the edge of the driver's side door.

He looked casually in-control. And all of a sudden, she knew why Stella's appealed to her. It would be her own space, her own gallery. She could display her own art and nurture other local artists. She'd be in control for the first time in oh-so-long. But she'd be living here, with a casual coastal lifestyle that was worlds away from the hustle and bustle of the Houston metropolis.

"So, you're thinking seriously about Stella's?" Spencer turned off the highway and into the area where Eve's beach house stood.

"Very. I want it."

Eve surprised herself by being so confident. But this...she just *knew*. She didn't know how she knew, but her heart and her soul pulled her along, telling her this one wasn't up for debate.

"Wow." Spencer pulled the Jeep into its spot under the house's pilings.

"What?" Eve couldn't quite tell if that was a good *wow* or a bad *wow*. "You don't think I can do it?"

Spencer hopped out and came around to open Eve's door. "Quite the opposite. I hear the passion in your voice, even in the few words you've said. You're involved with a gallery now, but all the responsibilities will now be solely on you...will that impact your creativity and your ability to paint?"

Eve nodded slowly. "I know I can manage this. My mom and I used to talk about it all the time. "There's something inside that is just telling me this is meant to be."

"I've always believed that when God puts a dream in your heart, it's there for a reason, just waiting for the right time to grow."

Funny, she'd certainly never heard Mark talk about God. He didn't believe in a higher power. He only believed in himself.

But for her own purposes, Eve had pretty much stopped putting much faith in God after she watched her mother die slowly followed by Mark stomping on what was left of her heart.

"Spencer, this isn't some divine miracle. We just happened to be in the right place at the right time."

"Evie, there are no coincidences. You told me you planned to spend New Year's alone in the beach house. But you're also telling me that taking over Stella's meant to be. Both of those are completely opposite. If you'd done what you insisted you've been planning for months, you'd never have known about this opportunity that could change your whole life."

The light blue of Spencer's eyes reminded Eve of frost, and a sudden chill shimmied down her spine. She felt the touch of the realization as it crossed every vertebrae.

Without Spencer coming to the beach, she could have missed out on this chance.

A single ray of sun poked through a gap between the deck boards above. It cast a glow on Spencer's face. What else would Eve have missed out on if he hadn't shown up yesterday afternoon?

This.

She'd have missed out on this. She'd have missed out on that kiss on the street in front of Stella's. She'd have missed out on unearthing a dose of emotion she didn't even know she still harbored inside.

"I stopped trusting myself, Spencer."

He smiled, and Eve felt her breath catching in her throat.

"'The best laid plans of mice and men often go astray.'"

Eve tried to give Spencer her best cheeky side-eye. "I'm not sure if I like being compared to a rodent."

Spencer laughed and put his hand on her shoulder with a squeeze. "The legendary poet Robbie Burns first said that. You know what other poem he wrote?"

Eve shook her head. She remembered learning about Burns in school, but that had been more years back than she cared to own up to.

"Auld Lang Syne."

"Isn't that about New Year's?"

"It will be quoted more times tonight than any other night of the year. Burns asked if it was right to forget the times in the past. Evie, you can't forget the past. But you also can't lock yourself into what you think your destiny is." He let his arm slide down, and adjusted his position so he was facing her, then Spencer took Eve's hands in his own. "Promise me something," he said.

Eve pressed her lips together, pulling them between her teeth and squeezing. She pulled a steadying draw of air in through her nose. "Okay?"

She feared he'd give her a dare, something crazy she couldn't—or wouldn't—deliver on.

But, the voice in the back of her head reminded her of one thing. Spencer hadn't been wrong. She owed it to him—and to herself—to hear him out.

"Don't box yourself in. Don't cut yourself off. You weren't made to spend a New Year's Eve in isolation. You were made to shine every bit as brightly as the fireworks they'll be shooting off tonight."

Even with all the enthusiasm she'd had for the gallery since the moment she'd stepped inside, Eve wished she held even one-tenth of the certainty that Spencer clearly did.

"I know you mean well, Spencer. And I know I can do this. But..."

The one thing she didn't know was how to tell him just how right he was about her. He could see the war in her heart and he called it for what it was.

"But what?" He gave her hands a gentle squeeze.

Eve kicked at a rock near her toes, then shook her head.

"Get in the car, Evie."

She felt her eyes grow wide. "What?"

"Get back in the Jeep, Eve. We're going back downtown. You're going to sign papers on Stella's right now before you talk yourself out of it. There's still plenty I need to know in life, but one thing I do know is a good business deal. And I think I know a little bit about you—although I'd like to know more, if you'll let me. But we'll take care of that part later."

Spencer lifted their clasped hands as he leaned down to place a soft kiss just below her knuckles. "You're starting to overthink it and you'll have yourself talked out of it by morning. You came down here so you could make a fresh start and put a line in the sand between your old life and your new life, right?"

Eve nodded. "Mm-hmm."

"Then we're getting in the car. You're doing this, Eve. This is your year. Shine, Evie. You deserve it."

Spencer stood a few steps away from the front counter in Stella's, taking in the scene as Eve picked up a ballpoint pen and signed a letter of intent to start the process to buy the Stella's by the Shore gallery in the heart of Port Provident's tourist district.

For a split second, Spencer's thoughts flashed back to Mark's fury on the sidewalk earlier. Spencer started to feel his own anger begin to rise again just at the memory. But then, in his mind's eye, he saw Eve step forward and dig deep and find the courage to say to Mark what she'd been holding inside for months.

It took guts to face down your adversary.

It took steel to say everything you meant to say.

Spencer had sat across from numerous so-called big-shots over the years. But rarely had he been impressed with anyone like he had been with Eve this afternoon.

She didn't give herself enough credit.

She could hang in the biggest boardroom and hold her own.

And if he was honest, she was already holding her own in Spencer's thoughts...and his heart.

How had all of this changed so quickly?

He'd always liked Eve. He'd been excited to have her as a sister-in-law. She came across as the calm to Mark's high-powered emotional storm. Spencer thought of Eve as a balancing influence, and anyone who could keep Mark in check made Spencer's own life easier. So for that reason alone, he'd admired her for a long time.

And for the last year, he'd thought about her from time to time, especially as Mark paraded his new trophy girlfriend around. Every so often, Spencer would wonder where Eve was and how she was doing, but he'd never gone the step further to reach out.

He regretted that now.

How much time had he missed?

How much could he have helped Eve when she needed a friend? When she needed a shoulder to lean on. He knew of her mom's cancer diagnosis, but not of her death.

He could do better.

He would do better now.

After all, it wasn't just a new year for Eve, it was a new year for him too.

It would be a new year where he stepped out of Mark's shadow, took charge of his health, and charted a new course.

And for now, that course had led him to Port Provident. It led him to Eve. And it led him to this moment in Stella's cheerful gallery where he had the opportunity to support a good woman who deserved a hope and a future.

Spencer felt the corner of his mouth turn up as he remembered the conversation by the Jeep about an hour before. He didn't believe in coincidence.

Being here with Eve...it was meant to be.

Now, he just needed to figure out why.

"Spencer!" Stella's throaty laugh cut like a knife into the inner dialogue he'd been having with himself. "Come over here and get a photo of Eve as she signs the paper. That way, we can put it up on social media."

With a speed in his step that he hadn't noticed for months, Spencer came closer to the edge of the counter. He pulled his phone out of his pocket and held it up, trying to get Stella and Eve in the shot. Both women smiled broadly. He could see the relief in Stella's face. He had felt that way more than once as a contract got signed.

As he re-sized the photo on the screen of his camera with a pinch of his fingers, Spencer turned all his attention on Eve's smile. He wanted to see if it was genuine.

Her lips curved up in a sweet half-moon. Only a trace of her lipstick remained, but she didn't need it anyway. She radiated a natural beauty that only confidence could bring out.

Spencer loved seeing the real Eve. The camera didn't do her justice.

"I'm going to see to it that you keep that smile on your face, Eve," Spencer said as he tapped the dot on the screen for one last photo. "You're going to do great things here."

Stella nodded in agreement. "Oh, yes. This is such a special location. I'm excited to be moving closer to my grandbabies, but I'll miss it here so much. Your online portfolio looks perfect for the market down here."

She took two steps back and picked up a little frame displayed next to the register. "I want you to have this."

Stella handed the little three-by-three square to Eve and patted it in a gesture of farewell.

"'I know the plans I have for you, plans to prosper you and not to harm you, plans to give you a hope and a future.'" Eve read the words, then looked up at Stella.

"That's my favorite Bible verse. It's very personal to a lot of people, because I think we can all see ourselves in it. But it was originally spoken to a group of Isrealites in exile. They were waiting to come home, waiting for their next opportunity. Your future is here, Eve. Welcome home."

"I made a lot of plans for this New Year's," Eve said, letting her words trail off as she looked up at the stars.

"I thought you hadn't made any plans?" Spencer wrapped an arm around her shoulders. Eve was grateful for the additional warmth, as a coastal chill had settled into the air once the sun went down.

"Well, I did and I didn't, I guess. I didn't buy a ticket to any parties, but I knew how I wanted today to go. I'd braced myself for certain feelings. And nothing's gone as I expected."

Spencer tilted his head. "I thought you were excited about Stella's."

Eve couldn't keep the smile from her face. "I am. That's exactly what I mean. I didn't expect to be excited. I expected to be all somber and closed off. Nothing has gone to plan, and I don't think I could be any happier."

"Me neither," Spencer said, as he turned Eve in his arms. "I don't think I want the calendar to change."

A crack and boom filled the air around them. Eve kept her focus on Spencer. The fireworks were starting, and midnight was at hand. But what was he talking about?

"You don't? Are you having second thoughts about quitting your job?"

Spencer began to laugh. "The only thing I'm second-guessing is why I didn't tell off Mark sooner."

"So what is it?" Curiosity hummed in Eve's brain like a hive of bees.

"Tomorrow is back to reality. The car will be fixed. I'll need to go back home. You have a gallery to pull together."

If Eve didn't know better, she'd say Spencer sounded defeated.

"Why don't you stay, Spencer?"

His head perked up. For a split-second, she saw the child he'd been so long ago. "Where? Here?"

"Well, maybe not here-here. That probably wouldn't work. But there are tons of rentals on the island. Why don't you get something on the island and regroup after your exit from Canley Communications."

For a second, the pop-pop-pop of fireworks ceased. Only the roar of the waves a few hundred yards away hung between them.

This was the moment she'd been waiting for this whole past year. Not the physical shift of time and the flip of the calendar.

Eve knew that now.

She'd been waiting for the chance to connect with someone. Someone who cared what she thought, what she said, what she did.

She'd been waiting for the fireworks—not in the sky, but in her bruised and battered heart.

But how could she hold something as fleeting and elusive as a firefly? A wish, a whisper, a spark?

Perhaps the truth.

Maybe the simple, heartfelt truth. She decided to try it. It was all she had.

"I'd like you to stay."

Eve felt the negative pressure in her lungs as she exhaled. She couldn't take another breath back in until Spencer answered.

"Why?" he asked. His eyes locked on hers. She could feel his gaze searching hers. He'd know if she wasn't telling the truth.

"I know about galleries, but not about business." She should have just left it there. He would have understood exactly what she meant. But more truth pulled out of her, almost as though Spencer were a magnet attracting her thoughts. "And I know what it means to follow a Canley brother and to hate a Canley brother. I'd like to know what it's like to enjoy being around one."

Spencer kept his thoughts closed.

Eve began to feel light-headed. She'd made herself vulnerable, but it wasn't working. Stella's favorite verse clearly had not been meant for Eve. In her own way, she'd asked Spencer for hope and a future.

And none was given in return.

Slowly, Spencer pulled her toward him. A dazzling display lit up the sky. Cracks and bangs filled the air.

Midnight.

"Make a wish, Eve," Spencer said, with his face just inches from hers. "And I will be here next year. You can tell me if it came true."

He touched his lips to hers, suddenly bringing the intensity of the fireworks to every nerve and vein in her body. She could feel Spencer's promise in her soul.

New Year's was here. She thought she'd known what she wanted.

Now she wanted more.

Maybe she'd been wrong about Stella's verse. As Spencer ended the kiss, Eve looked up at the sky and thoughts began to collect, and a prayer slipped through her mind.

I've never done this before...but if You're out there...could this be the year that my hope for something better turns into a brighter future? I never knew I was waiting for Spencer. But maybe You did? Maybe I've been chasing the wrong dream. Show me the New Year's resolution I should have been dreaming about.

This time, she wasn't focused on the shooting arches decorating the black overhead. She looked at the stars. She looked for Heaven. She looked for hope.

Maybe this would be the year she found something she never knew she needed.

Chapter Seven

Spencer couldn't believe he and Eve had found a day off. The two of them had worked almost non-stop for weeks, trying to get the gallery, now named Eve Inspirations, ready for a grand opening.

Eve had so many ideas to ensure the success of her new venture. And she'd challenged herself at every turn. She'd done things completely outside of her comfort zone—setting up inventory tracking systems and accounting software and insurance policies.

Spencer was proud of her drive and her determination. But it worried him a bit too. Since he came to Port Provident that afternoon before New Year's Eve, Eve had not painted—not even one single brush stroke.

Every time she spoke about painting or light or seeing a certain scene a certain way, a sparkle circled the edges of her hazel irises—like a twinkle of ice on a fresh winter morning. And today, Spencer planned to bring that glimmer back.

But first...he had to get her out of the gallery.

Spencer swung the Jeep into a parallel parking space directly in front of the gallery's main door. The new Eve Inspirations Gallery sign had been hung yesterday, a glossy custom wooden sign with a soaring seagull logo Eve had sketched herself.

From the outside, everything looked ready to go. It wouldn't be long now. Which is why Spencer knew he had to get Eve out from the walls of the gallery and back in her creative zone. Once Eve Inspirations opened, things would be hectic for a while.

But not today.

Today would be a day for them to simply *be*.

Together.

"I hope you brought lunch," Eve said as Spencer walked through the door. "I think they can hear my stomach growling next door at the Jewelry Box."

"Better," Spencer said as he smiled at the sight of her. "I'm bringing you to lunch."

Eve shook her head. "I can't leave. The interior designer is bringing light fixtures by today. I have to select them this week."

"You do—but today's not that day. I already called her and moved the appointment to tomorrow."

Eve pushed stray locks of hair back from the top of her forehead. "Spencer, you can't do that. We have a schedule."

"Well, now you sound like me. That proves I'm right. We can't have you starting to sound like a buttoned-up lawyer. You're an artist. You need to get back to thinking like an artist, or you won't have anything to hang on the walls here once your first collection sells out—and I believe that's going to happen soon."

Eve looked around the walls. "I do need more inventory. What if someone wants something that's not here?"

Spencer wrapped his arms around her and squeezed, feeling every curve and line of her body next to him. Holding her like this felt right, but if they stayed too long, they'd miss the light at the Point and the lighthouse that had guided generations of people to Port Provident. "Then you're going to give it to them. So, we've got to get you out of these four walls and back to nature."

"Lead the way," Eve said, snuggling even more deeply into their embrace.

Spencer decided a small detour wouldn't hurt. "Maybe in a few minutes. I feel inspired, myself, right now."

Keeping his arms wrapped closely around Eve's shoulders, Spencer leaned down and kissed her, then kissed her some more as the sun's rays began to flood the gallery's interior and shine brightly.

"You're the artist...if a picture is worth a thousand words," Spencer murmured as his lips trailed down the slope of Eve's neck, "what do you suppose a kiss is worth?"

"I'm not exactly sure. But if you kiss me again, I'll let you know."

Spencer kissed his way back up the gentle lines of Eve's neck. "We can do as much research as you need."

Spencer leaned back, resting on his elbows atop a blanket he'd thrown over the poky grass a few hundred yards from the lighthouse. A Port Provident landmark, the Point Provident lighthouse stood cheerfully decked in red and white stripes. A light at the top took lazy three-hundred-and-sixty degree spins, surveying all the island and the Gulf of Mexico beyond had to offer. Not too far in the distance was the smaller island of Provident Cay, owned by five local friends who set up the global headquarters of their internationally-recognized cybersecurity company on the private setting.

But Spencer only had eyes for Eve.

And Eve only had eyes for her canvas.

Her brush laid down bold strokes, then tempered those sections of color with delicate details. It fascinated him to watch how she created something out of virtually nothing.

He remembered childhood Sunday school stories of God creating the universe from a void. In her own way, Eve was following that same hallowed tradition.

Eve swiveled around on her stool, looking back at Spencer as she reached for another color of paint from her box. "What'cha thinking about?"

"Honestly?" He and Eve had never really discussed faith and he knew she'd never been to church with Mark...because, well, Mark believed in no power higher than himself.

Eve laughed. "Of course. Honestly."

"God," Spencer said simply.

She turned around and began to paint again. Spencer worried that he'd offended her in some way. He certainly wouldn't apologize for his beliefs, but at the same time, today was supposed to be calming, relaxing. It wasn't a day for differences.

"I didn't see that coming," she said softly.

"I've had a lot of time to consider my own mortality the last few months," Spencer explained. "Dealing with heart issues makes you stop and think."

Eve continued to sweep her brush across the canvas. "I know. It made you realize you didn't want to be a part of Canley Communications anymore."

"And that I wanted to be with you," Spencer affirmed. He'd learned so much about himself since the middle of last year.

What he didn't want in his life anymore.

And most importantly, what—and who—he did want.

"There are churches all over Port Provident. I'm sure you could find one that suits you."

That seemed like a good idea to Spencer. If he was going to truly call Port Provident home, he needed to plug in at different levels, find his connections in the community.

But he didn't want to do any of that alone.

"Would you come with me?"

Eve stopped painting, her brush hovering mid-stroke at a red strip near the top of the lighthouse. He could hear a sharp intake of breath above the sounds of the sea breeze. "I don't know, Spencer. I haven't set foot in a church since my mom's funeral."

Slowly and deliberately, she began to paint again. Spencer watched her hand move and dab a little bit of white here and there over the scene she'd created.

"That. What you're doing there."

"Huh?" Eve cast a glance back over her shoulder.

"You're bringing light to the dark spots."

Eve nodded. "Yeah. This landscape can't be too dark. There were some shadows."

"The same is true for you, you know. We all have shadows. But what we need is light. And love." Spencer raised himself off the blanket and began to walk toward the woman who had quickly captured his whole heart. "Come with me."

Deliberately, Eve swiped a swish of white at the edge of the lighthouse, giving the painting a depth and dimension that hadn't been there only seconds before.

She inhaled again, then exhaled.

Spencer couldn't tell what her answer would be. He wasn't sure if Eve herself knew what she would say.

"Light and love, right?" She spoke softly, but Spencer could hear a shy smile behind the words.

Spencer nodded, feeling the golden rays of the island sunshine on his skin.

"I could use both," Eve acknowledged.

He put out his hand, and Eve placed her palm atop his. He gave a gentle tug upward, and she stood. With a small shuffle, Spencer cut the space between them by half. He intended to close it fully, to take her in his arms and show her without words what his true thoughts were—but he had something he needed to say first.

"You already have love, Eve. I love you. There's no doubt in my mind or my heart."

The Sunday morning light cut crisply through the sheer curtains in Eve's bedroom. She rolled over and looked at the red numbers on the clock on the small table only an arm's length away. Spencer would be here in an hour to pick her up.

And then she'd have to face her fears.

Eve flopped back on her back, staring at the ceiling above. Somewhere on the other side of that ceiling was God. He was probably looking at her right this minute—knowing how uncomfortable she was.

Did He know how much she regretted telling Spencer she would go with him to a service at First Provident Church this morning?

Did that make Him angry to know she would rather do just about anything else this morning than set foot in a church?

Or did He not even care?

Because that's how their relationship had gone for years.

No God who truly cared would have left her alone to face the last two years. From finding out that her mother had cancer, to watching her die day by day—and then finally losing her for good, to Mark's humiliating betrayal, to the year she spent basically alone and adrift, trying to find a renewed life's purpose...

No God who was good would have stood by and watched as Eve's heart broke over and over again.

And she'd told him so on the day of her mother's funeral.

Then Eve never looked back.

Until today. Now, she was stuck looking up. Her eyes focused on the popcorn ceiling above her. She contemplated every single little stark white bump.

It passed the time because Eve knew she wasn't ready to get out of bed. She wasn't ready to shower. And even though she'd uttered that short, quiet prayer as the fireworks rocketed across the sky on New Year's Eve, she wasn't ready for each and every minute that would get her closer to the door of First Provident.

Slowly, she willed herself to sit up and get out of bed.

God may have let her down, she thought, rolling her eyes upward for emphasis. But she would not let Spencer down.

"Eve, you're really quiet this morning," Spencer said as he turned his sports car onto the main road that would take them back into town from the beachside neighborhood at the far end of the island where Eve lived.

"Hmm?" She continued to stare out the car window as beach house after beach house whooshed by.

"Are you okay?" Spencer's voice was filled with concern.

Eve didn't quite know how to answer him. Physically, she felt fine.

But mentally?

She was living on another planet right now.

"Sure. I mean, I guess so."

Well, that answer wasn't convincing at all. She didn't fool herself. She definitely wasn't going to fool Spencer.

"Yeah, totally not convinced, Eve."

Ugh. It was as though he could read her mind. Normally, she loved that. It made her feel in sync with Spencer—like they truly understood each other.

But right now...no.

"I don't even really understand myself right now. I can't really expect you to."

"Try me." Spencer turned and smiled as he slowed down for a stop light just ahead. "You know I'll help if I can."

His calm voice petted her nerves like a gentle grandmother with a favorite cat. She needed to trust him. If she couldn't be honest with him about the hard things, then she was wrong about how in sync they truly were.

"It's church. I don't want to go."

There. She said it. Just dumped it all out there like a truckload of sand brought to create a dune.

"Okay. But why?"

Eve turned back toward the window. She simply couldn't make eye contact *and* say everything she needed to say right now.

"I just..." This was hard. "I just can't see how God's really in my life. I think he forgot about me. My mom is gone—she suffered...I suffered. And then Mark...and that whole lost year until you showed up. I know I'm not explaining it very well. It's all a mess in my head and my heart and my words. But it's still my mess. And it's been really lonely. God hasn't been there, Spencer."

Silence settled in the car for a moment.

Eve felt her skin began to itch. Was she breaking out in hives? That would just be the icing on the cake. Now she would be full of nerves and visible splotches. The congregation would see her coming a mile away.

Spencer tapped Eve on the shoulder. She turned her head and looked at him, expecting to see disapproval on his face. He had been excited about going to church. He wouldn't be struggling with anything similar to what had filled her mind all morning.

He put his hand out to her, palm upward.

She searched his expression. His mouth curved, lifted at the edges. The gentle shift rounded his cheeks slightly and made the corners of his eyelids wrinkle just a bit.

Eve laid one hand on top of Spencer's. It felt as warm and affectionate as the look on his face.

He squeezed lightly as he continued to drive, turning through the streets of Port Provident. "I understand. Church is hard for me too, sometimes. You pull up and everyone's tried to look their best and behave their best. But every single one of those people is struggling with something. Every one of them is imperfect. You're no different than me or anyone else in there—wanting to be our best and knowing we fall short. Looking for grace."

"A little grace sounds good right about now."

"You deserve it. And honestly, Eve, you already have it—you just need to experience it for yourself." The softness on his face melted into a full smile. "And I'll be there with you, holding your hand, and looking for grace myself."

"But you sound so confident about it—you're not nervous or second-guessing your decisions."

"I second-guess myself all the time. I worked for Mark, remember? Then I quit...without an income or Plan B. Now I'm setting up my investment firm, but I've never been on my own like this before without my brothers. And I'm helping you with the gallery—but I wonder all the time if my advice is right, since I don't know anything about art. And then there's my health. It's always in the back of my mind, wondering if today is going to be the day that my heart condition goes haywire and changes everything in my life." Spencer turned the car into the parking lot at First Provident Church. "The only thing I don't second guess is you. You and me."

"I don't second guess that either." Eve felt stronger as she affirmed that one truth in her life. "And I don't want to live a life without hope. So maybe right here is where I need to be."

"'Surely goodness and mercy will follow me all the days of my life.' That's Psalm twenty-three six." Spencer raised their clasped hands and placed a gentle kiss on Eve's skin. A warmth puddled quickly through her body at the touch. "I have to live with the belief that good things will happen, Eve—because the alternative is too empty and lonely. Us, together, even with all of our crazy history, is one of the good things. You are one of those good things in my life—and mercy and grace are here for you too. Ready to go in and find out why?"

Eve nodded. In a year where she was starting everything over, she knew this was a fresh beginning she needed to make too. She would do this with Spencer, and she believed it would lead to better days ahead.

"It sounds so good to think of days with goodness and mercy following you and me around every corner of life, no matter where the journey takes us. I've run away from it for so long—believing that because so many bad things happened to me that I no longer deserved any better."

"You deserve the sun and the moon and the stars, Eve Larson." Spencer found a space for the car and shifted into park. "And the One who created all of those is waiting right inside. I'll be there every step of the way."

"I'm ready to go inside," she said, and all the doubts Eve had been holding tight inside for years washed away just like the tide that rolled only a few blocks away.

"And that's that." Matt McGregor signed his name on the contract with a flourish. "I think that means the three of us are business partners now."

Jake Peoples, Matt's cousin, picked up the papers and the pen. "I've spent a lot of time with real estate on this island, but I don't think I've ever been more excited about an opportunity. Really excited about the work Canley Investments is going to be doing on the island."

Spencer picked up his glass of iced tea for a mock toast. "Things are mostly back to normal around here after Hurricane Hope, but I am looking forward to making things better than normal. By buying old, distressed homes and bringing them back to life, we're not just going to be preserving history and changing the face of the island, but we're going to be providing affordable housing for people too. It feels like this is a business venture with a much bigger purpose."

Matt picked up a chilled shrimp off the bed of ice on the appetizer plate in the middle of the table, then dunked the pink half-curve in cocktail sauce.

"I agree. When we did this in San Petro last year, it surprised me that it made a noticeable difference in the community so quickly. But Annie told me that it would, and as usual, her heart didn't steer her wrong."

Matt was married to the Crown Princess of San Petro, a kingdom on a tropical Caribbean island. Port Provident and Rosada, San Petro's capital were sister cities, and after Hurricane Hope, Princess Anneliese came to Texas to lend a helping hand—and met Matt, who was leading an effort to rebuild one hundred homes in Port Provident's neighborhoods. A royal wedding soon followed, but Matt's family was anchored in Port Provident, and he remained connected to his hometown in many ways.

Spencer hoped his ties to Port Provident would, in time, become equally strong.

"How's everything going with the gallery?" Jake helped himself to the oversized appetizer as well.

Spencer couldn't keep from smiling. "We open officially next week. Eve's pulled a lot of late nights and worked pretty much non-stop to pull this off. I can't wait to see how the community responds. I hope there are Eve Inspirations original paintings in half the beach houses on Provident Island soon."

Jake nodded. "We have a blank wall at the office that bothers me. I'll stop by the gallery soon and pick out a painting."

"That's great, man. We'll make sure it's Nana-approved." Jake's grandmother, Diana Peoples, was the unofficial matriarch of the island. From charity to church to education to development, there wasn't an area of Port Provident that Diana's guidance and support didn't touch.

"Sounds good." Jake glanced down at his menu as he continued talking. "It was good to see you and Eve again at First Provident last week. That's what? Three weeks in a row?"

"Four," Spencer corrected.

"My uncle chairs the deacon committee. Watch out for a phone call soon. You're practically members now."

Spencer laughed. "I'd be okay with that. I even think Eve would be too. Just let us get the gallery open first."

"Totally understand," Jake said.

Matt reached for the basket of warm, crusty bread. "But don't wait too long. You're going to need that membership pretty soon."

Spencer eyed his friend carefully. He hadn't shared his heart condition diagnosis with anyone outside of Eve and a few members of his family. How did Matt know?

"Not sure I know what you mean, Matt."

"Come on. Don't you hear wedding bells in your future? I never thought I was cut out for marriage. And being up to my ears in sawdust and drywall all day—I certainly never thought

I'd get involved with a princess. But as I got to know Annie, none of that mattered. I just knew. I've seen you with Eve. I think you know exactly what I'm talking about."

Spencer's breathing slowed back to a more normal rate. "I won't lie. I've thought about it. Probably more than I should. But she was my brother's fiancée. What if my ring doesn't match up? Or my proposal? Or something else entirely?"

He couldn't believe he'd come out and said what had been poking at the back of his mind for weeks, since he first realized he'd fallen for Eve. But the words had come out and now he couldn't take them back—even though he cringed a bit inside at how stupid he sounded speaking them out loud.

"I saw you two last Sunday at church," Jake said. "She wasn't thinking about Mark. Trust me. It was obvious."

Matt nodded in agreement. "I remain grateful for the partnership that Canley Communications always showed Helping Hands Homes in getting internet and cable and phone to the families that we build for. But I've been in enough meetings with you and Mark both. I think I know both of you pretty well. And trust me, Eve is well rid of him—and she's smart enough to know it. You know it too."

Spencer looked at Jake and Matt across the table. Both of them wore flat expressions that conveyed total seriousness. They weren't just saying what Spencer wanted to hear.

"You're right, and I know you are. But sometimes that voice in the back of my head gets loud."

"Well, it's time to tell it to shut up," Matt said. "Eve is opening her dream gallery. You've started an investment firm to put your business skills to good use strengthening this community. Mark is out of the picture. Quit letting him back in. He isn't worth it."

Everything Matt said made far too much sense. "So, then, I've got a question for you both."

"Ask away," Jake said.

Spencer smiled. "Where's the best place in town to buy a ring?"

Chapter Eight

"Can you believe it?" Eve stood in the center of the room and turned her head, slowly scanning the room from left to right.

Spencer walked behind her and wrapped his arms around her waist, then leaned over and gave her a small kiss at the base of her neck. "You did it."

Eve shook her head. "No. We did it. This was a team project. There's no way that Eve Inspirations Gallery comes together without you. You encouraged me to do it. You called your friend at the bank to help me with the financing. And you've been here every single day for the last two months, writing the contracts for the other artists on display—and doing a little painting of your own. That back wall looks great, Spence."

Spencer couldn't help but chuckle. "You've seen the heights of my artistic talent here. I prefer to work in the exclusive medium of semi-gloss and paint roller."

"A man of discerning tastes," Eve said, turning her head toward him with a wink and a wide smile.

He spun her in his arms. "I picked you, didn't I?"

"I think we picked each other." The smile didn't leave her face as she spoke. It was like liquid sunshine for his soul. Spencer had been an arm's-length guy when it came to relationships. He never wanted to be all-in. But New Year's Eve had changed all that.

"Then we both have discerning tastes," he clarified.

"We do."

All he wanted to taste was her kiss. Spencer leaned in and took his time. He breathed in the scent of her, a light gardenia floral that suited her perfectly.

And he could have missed it all. If Mark hadn't been such a total jerk. If Spencer had quit one day sooner and not taken the letter. If any one of a hundred small things had gone a different way, this year would have been completely different for him and for Eve.

Gratitude overtook Spencer as he drew the kiss to a close.

"Thank you," he whispered, before realizing his thoughts had formed out loud.

Eve stepped back and sized him up with a quirk of her eyebrow. "For what?"

Spencer gave a short laugh. "Not you."

"Wait. You just kissed me. Now you're thanking someone else? Spencer...is there something I need to know about?"

He pulled her toward him again. This time, he just held her tightly, enjoying the feel of her close to him. "I told you way back at New Year's that I didn't believe in coincidences."

"Right." Eve craned her neck backward so she could keep his face in view.

"I still don't. I believe my car died in your driveway for a reason. I believe we're meant to be here together right now. And I'm thankful. God crossed our paths. I needed a new direction in my life, but I never knew the road would lead me to you. I knew this year needed to be different, but love was not a resolution I ever planned on making."

"Me neither. I thought I was done with all that."

"Aren't you glad you're not?"

Her smile was sincere. The glow around her face melted his soul. "Absolutely. We stood right here when Stella talked about a hope and a future. I didn't know this was the future I was meant to have. But here I am, with my own business—and a partner in everything."

"Your mom would be so proud of you, Eve," Spencer said, threading a finger underneath the pendant lying just at the top of her breastbone.

Eve touched the Kiss of Kiev diamond. "She would. Thank you for making it possible."

"You're the artist, Eve. You made your dream come true. Now, let's get ready for your grand opening."

Tonight, artists and collectors from the island and the mainland would come in here and see everything Eve had poured her spirit and her creativity into—works of art that would be destined for homes and boardrooms and the parlors of B&Bs.

But while everyone else's eyes would be on the canvases hanging on the wall, Spencer knew the most beautiful work of art in here tonight was Eve. And he couldn't wait to watch her shine.

The whole evening seemed magical. Maybe it was because today was leap year—a rare event on the calendar. But Eve didn't think so. She could feel her mother's spirit in the room, and she could feel the warmth of Spencer's love.

Eve stopped herself short. They'd never said anything like that to each other, but Eve knew one thing for certain. She'd fallen in love with Spencer. In just a few short months, he'd become her best friend, her sounding board, her business mentor. He'd challenged her to think about things as far reaching on the spectrum as finances and faith.

She'd never put much stock in either before. As an artist, she always declared herself to be "not a math person." And faith...well, it hadn't been a part of her life growing up. Once her mother got sick, she'd lost what little she may have had.

But Spencer had changed that. And two weeks ago, he'd even talked her into coming with him to a Sunday service at First Provident Church.

Her knees knocked under her skirt as they walked through the oversized ivory-painted doors. But from the minute they'd sat in one of the long pews in the center section of the church, a peace came over her. It was the same peace she'd had when Stella had spoken of hope and it was the same peace she'd had on the deck at New Year's when Spencer kissed her and made her think of a bright future ahead.

She turned back toward the far corner of the room, where Spencer had been talking with an elderly couple he knew from Houston.

But one look at Spencer told her something was off.

He leaned up against the yellow-painted plaster wall with a faraway look in his eyes.

Eve smiled at the members of the group she'd been chatting with and tried to disengage herself. She needed to get back to Spencer.

As soon as she reached the back corner, she touched him lightly on the arm. His smile of acknowledgement seemed frustrated. The right edge of his mouth curled up slightly.

"Something's wrong," she said in a raised whisper after being introduced to the couple from Houston, who quickly turned back to studying a detailed watercolor of a seagull.

Spencer shook his head, but Eve didn't believe the wordless denial. "Just my A-Fib."

Eve felt her eyes go completely round. "Where are your meds?"

He'd only had one mild atrial fibrillation attack since moving to Port Provident, but just the idea of his heart acting up made Eve's blood turn to ice water.

"They're back at my condo. I'm fine."

Eve positioned herself between Spencer and the crowd. "You're not. Go back to the office and sit down for a minute. I've got this out here. Everyone's fine."

"So am I." Spencer tried to make his words sound strong, but Eve heard his breathing begin to quicken.

Eve opened her mouth to argue, but a familiar voice raised above the din of the conversation criss-crossing the groups of guests in the gallery.

"Eve Larson, this is for you."

Eve spun around and saw Mark Canley cutting through the crowd.

Spencer started to move, then fell back against the wall.

Mark handed an envelope to Eve and one to Spencer. "And this one is for you, Brother."

"Mark, what are you doing here?" Eve desperately wanted eyes in the back of her head to check on Spencer.

He hadn't said a word to Mark.

His silence terrified her.

"Serving you with papers. I knew you'd be here. My father mentioned Spencer's big night with his new little business."

Eve felt the coolness of the Kiss of Kiev in the necklace. It rested lightly on her chest. "Papers...for what?"

"My diamond. I'm taking you to court." He turned on his heel and addressed the gathering of gallery patrons. "She's a thief and a liar, folks. She's stolen my property. Who knows what she'll steal from you."

With that, Mark walked out, the sound of the heels of his dress shoes echoing loudly as they tapped the sealed concrete floor.

A bolt of lightning ran from Eve's forehead to the pit of her stomach. The entire room fell into silence. They'd all heard.

Mark had ruined her brand-new business with a handful of sentences.

Tightness squeezed Eve's throat from her jaw to her collarbone. She couldn't breathe.

A sound like sandpaper came from behind her.

Spencer slid down the wall and collapsed in a heap in the corner.

Everything inside of her screamed for someone to call 911.

But she had no words.

She had no hope.

She had no future.

Eve's year—the year that was supposed to be different—slipped away like the sand at the shoreline. And all she could do was watch as all her dreams faded into a palette of unending shades of gray like the sky before a coastal storm.

A constant beeping kept playing next to his head, but it didn't sound a darned thing like his alarm clock. Spencer tried to reach back to turn it off but couldn't stretch his arm very far. Rolling his head to the side, he saw tape covering the back of his hand where it held in an IV catheter. The catheter connected to clear tubing that snaked along the curve of his forearm.

Slowly, it dawned on him. The beeping was a cardiac monitor.

He wasn't at the gallery anymore.

The sign on the wall listed the core values of Provident Medical Center.

He'd been brought to the hospital.

"Spencer?"

His brother stood up from the chair in the corner and walked to the bed.

"Dave?" Spencer's voice cracked as the syllable struggled to come out. They must have needed to intubate him. "Was it bad?"

"Eve said you hit your head on a display shelf when you slid to the floor. It knocked you out cold, on top of fainting from the A-fib. They brought you back—you're lucky this place is two blocks from the gallery—but you're heading in for surgery tomorrow morning."

Surgery and what was to come didn't matter.

"Where's Eve?"

Dave's shadow angled across the stark white hospital sheets. "I sent her home."

A sudden surge of adrenaline made the cardiac monitor do double-time. "Why?"

Spencer felt dizzy all over again.

"She asked me to give you this."

Dave held out a small, ivory envelope. Spencer reached out to grab it, but a stabbing pain poked through the center of his hand. "Open it? Read it to me?"

He wished he could talk in complete sentences, but aside from the sandpaper in his throat, more syllables would only mean a longer delay to hear what Eve wanted him to know.

Dave laid the envelope on the bed, then opened the seal and pulled out the contents. Spencer tried to scan the brief note as the only brother he trusted unfolded the paper.

Dear Spencer,

I'm on my way to Mark's office now. I'm giving him the Kiss of Kiev. I don't want it anymore. I don't want the trouble attached to it. I should have chased him down the street on New Year's Eve and given it to him then—but you'd stood up for me and I didn't want that to be in vain. But now, because I didn't do what I needed to do when I had the chance, I caused you to almost lose your life. I know your atrial fibrillation is made worse by stress—and although we've done good work for a good cause, the last few weeks getting the gallery ready have been stressful for us both. And then to have Mark walk in like that—it was just too much. And it was all my fault. All of it. I'm going to fix this with Mark and pray that he leaves you alone once he gets what he wants from me. And then I'm going to stay away for a while. I can't cause you any more stress.

Thank you for everything. I'm sorry I caused this.

Love,

Eve

Of all that, Spencer only heard one thing. She'd signed it with "love." They'd never talked about it before, but Spencer knew he'd loved her from the moment she'd bravely handed over the necklace on that rainy day before New Year's Eve.

"What do you think?" Dave folded the note in half and handed it to Spencer.

Spencer waved it away. He didn't want to think about it. She obviously was using "love" in a standard greeting-card kind of way. If she truly loved him, she wouldn't be bowing out.

"I think she's gone," he said, letting out a breath and listening to the steady beep of the monitor behind him, realizing that no matter what the doctors did to him tomorrow morning, his heart would never be the same.

Not long after the calendar turned to March, signs of spring began to show on the island. Eve adjusted her easel in the corner window at the front of her store. Tourists seemed to love to stop and watch her paint. It brought a lot of traffic into the store and had turned into a few sales. All in all, Eve felt a deep sense of satisfaction at how the gallery was running.

But she couldn't escape the parallel deep sense of loss every time she thought of how the gallery was running. Spencer had set up all the operational logistics for the gallery. He was the reason the cash register connected to the bank account and the reason the ads were placed in local lifestyle magazines and the reason that she couldn't look at anything in this building and not think of him.

She had to force herself not to let her thoughts carry her away like a rip current, though. Leaving that note for Spencer had been the right decision—even if it was the toughest decision. Mark would always be a thorn in Spencer's side as long as she was a part of his life. She may have returned the Kiss of Kiev, but Mark wouldn't let it end there. He'd continue to jab at Spencer whenever he could that Spencer had picked up Mark's cast-off.

And Eve knew Spencer would always defend her. She loved him for that.

But it would just cause him stress. And stress would just lead to a continued life of heart problems. Eve knew in her own heart that she couldn't be the cause of anything that would negatively impact Spencer's health.

The bell over the door jingled and the face that walked in the gallery caused her to do a double-take. She knew those broad shoulders and the slight tilt of the head. She dreamed about the sound of that footfall.

Spencer?

Not Spencer.

David. The third Canley brother.

"Eve?" David walked toward her purposefully.

"Come in, David." Eve stood up from her stool in front of the easel. "I don't guess you're here to buy a coastal watercolor?"

David shook his head. "I'm here about Spencer."

A lump hopscotched into Eve's throat. It stuck there like an errant cactus. It was impossible to deny the prickly sense of awareness of the flood of dread that rushed through her body.

"Oh...no..." she fell heavily onto the stool as her legs buckled out from underneath her. Suddenly, she regretted that note. She should have told him in person. It would have been the hardest conversation she would ever undertake, but at least...at least she could have told him goodbye. "He's not...David, don't tell me he's..."

David crossed the floor in three steps and he braced Eve's arm with his palm. "No, not that. He's at his condo, resting. They discharged him yesterday. He doesn't know I'm here."

She slumped a little on the tiny stool.

"So why are you here?"

"Because I need to know. Why'd you leave him that letter?" His tone blended together equal parts of anger and questioning.

"I had to, David." She began to straighten brushes on the table next to her. She could barely explain what she felt inside to herself. How could she explain it to Spencer's best friend, the one brother with whom he still had an unbreakable bond?

"He barely eats. He says maybe ten sentences a day, Eve."

She tried to explain David's concern away logically. "He's just had heart surgery, David."

"He has a broken heart, Eve."

Eve swiveled on the stool. "We weren't really together that long, David."

"Long enough."

David had her there. It had been long enough for her to fall hard and dream of forever. Maybe it had been long enough for Spencer, too.

"I'm just trouble for him. Mark will never leave him alone as long as I'm around. He served him with a lawsuit for breach of contract."

"He's got a good lawyer, Eve. He's not in any danger there."

"Who?" Eve knew she had no business asking, but she couldn't deny her curiosity.

David shrugged, then smiled. "My dad. Mark's wrong. We all know it."

Eve nodded in agreement. "I gave him back the necklace. He just took it out of my hand without even talking to me."

"He's moving to Russia."

"He's what?" Eve dropped the paintbrush she'd been holding.

"Moving. Going to be closer to Svetlana's father. And his billions—and all those lucrative contracts." David stuck his hand in his pockets.

"So...are you running the company from here?"

David shook his head. "No. My last day with Canley Communications was February twenty-ninth."

"The night Spencer collapsed."

"It was the last straw."

"So, Mark's gone."

"And so, it seems, are you."

Eve didn't know what to say. But she knew there was something she needed to do.

Spencer's head jerked at the sound of the three knocks on the door. "Use your key, Dave."

A few seconds later, three more raps sounded.

"Just a minute," Spencer said as he pushed himself off the couch. He stepped on a fortune cookie wrapper as he slowly moved toward the door. The cellophane crackled under his feet, but he didn't stop to pick up the white scrap of paper with the pithy proclamation.

He knew what his fortune was now.

And he'd rather not think about it. A world without Eve was nothing but *mis*-fortune. But Eve had made her wishes clear. And no matter what it took, he'd respect them.

Mark hadn't respected her. Spencer promised he'd be the Canley brother who wouldn't let her down. He told her he was different. He couldn't go back on that.

He wouldn't.

Spencer flipped the lock and pulled the door open a crack.

A pair of toffee-glass eyes looked back at him and his heart began to rev like a race car at the starting line.

Spencer lifted his arm and pressed his hand to his chest, trying to feel for the sinus rhythm. "Eve?"

"Can I come in?"

He swung the door open. "Always."

"Thanks." Eve walked past him, and the scent of gardenias trailed gracefully into his condo.

Spencer pointed a hand toward the couch. The gesture seemed so awkward. They'd watched movies together on this couch. They'd shared take-out. They'd cuddled and talked about dreams and the future.

But now, the couch seemed to be reduced to a piece of furniture requiring a formal invitation for use.

Eve sat on the right-hand cushion of the couch. Spencer lowered himself to the left. One cushion held the space in between. It felt as wide as the Gulf of Mexico which stretched just past his balcony to the horizon beyond.

"The surgery went well?" Eve sounded unsure of herself.

Spencer knew exactly how she felt. He'd never been less sure of any conversation, including the one where he quit his role at Canley Communications.

He raised his hand back to his chest, quietly counting the thumps. "It did. I was in there about twice as long as they thought it would take, but my doctor thinks he got the right spot. The ablation kills the abnormal cells so they don't beat out of rhythm anymore."

"No episodes since then?"

"Not unless I have one right now." He decided to bite the bullet. Small talk wasn't going to suit his recovery. "Why are you here, Eve?"

She bit her lip and the shine in her eyes went dull. "Because I was wrong."

Spencer didn't know what to say, so he kept quiet and let Eve keep talking.

"I was so scared. I held your hand and waited for the paramedics. I thought I was going to lose you. Actually, I didn't think. I knew it. And it would have been my fault. I was the reason Mark was there. I would have been the reason you died. As I waited for the sirens and the paramedics, I tried to tell you goodbye, but I couldn't. So I started to pray. And I told God that if He'd just let you live, I'd go away. We'd talked so much about the future, but I wasn't the future you needed. A future with me would just bring stress and strife into your life. You'd find love again, but with someone who didn't have all the Mark-baggage. I was just babbling in my head to God, but it made sense to me at the time. And then you lived, so I had to honor all those promises I'd made and words I'd said."

"Evie, that isn't how it works. God's got the hope and the future. Not us. We don't know where it will take us. We go on the journey with Him. And we trust and grow in faith. People are always coming in and out of our lives. You came into mine. Mark went out. He's not my future. You are. Would I like to reconcile with my brother some day? Sure. I'll be praying for him until the day I die. But I pray for you, too. For us."

A single tear rolled down her cheek. He wanted to reach out and smooth it away.

Spencer figured he didn't have anything to lose. He scooted to the middle cushion and raised his arm, touching his thumb to the curve just below her eyes. He wiped the liquid away and wished he could just as easily wipe the recent past away.

"For us?"

Another tear began to roll. This time, Spencer smoothed it without hesitation.

"For us."

She reached out a tentative hand. Spencer clasped her palm between both of his own.

"I love you, Spencer. I used to have so many plans, so many dreams of what I needed to do with my life to be at peace with myself and where I'd been. But the only future I want now is one with you in it."

Spencer pulled Eve close. He felt his heart begin to beat faster, staying in a clear, perfect rhythm.

Just before he leaned down to claim a kiss to lay to rest all the scares and misunderstandings that had come between him, he paused. "I love you, Evie. Loving you was the best New Year's resolution I ever made."

Epilogue

Walking down the hall at Port Provident High School felt a little strange. Eve loved everything about art, but this was the first time she'd ever been asked to paint a public mural. Covering the length of the main hallway, it was the largest project she'd ever worked on.

Months of time and effort had gone into this project. And now, at the start of the new school year, the entire project would be revealed to the school, education leaders, and others of note in the Port Provident community.

Eve had gotten to know many of the teachers at Port Provident High School while she'd worked on the project. Each area of the school was represented on the wall—from classic Shakespeare in the English department, to a scene depicting the stage in honor of the Theatre department, and even a nod to the district's new science and technology-focused high school, which celebrated its grand opening last week.

Taking a step back, Eve looked at the full project and smiled.

"I love everything about this! Look how phenomenal our little Globe Theatre looks." Amanda Marsh, Eve's long-time friend and the high school's English teacher, beamed at her section of the hallway art.

"The way you have the door to your classroom styled was a huge inspiration. You're very artistic yourself."

Amanda beamed. "It's half the fun of teaching—making traditional ideas and things to be taught come alive for the kids in new and different ways."

"I'd definitely say you're winning in that area." Eve stopped next to her new friend. She'd come to love Amanda's passion for literature, teaching, and her students. "I would have loved to have learned in a classroom like yours."

Amanda pointed at Eve's bag of art supplies. "And I would love to spend time learning to paint in a studio like yours."

Eve pulled out her phone and waved it at her friend. "You know where to find me. Maybe this fall we could do some sessions."

"I would love that," Amanda said, tucking the card inside of her rainbow-striped teacher's planner. "I can't believe we are already starting a new school year and celebrating our first pep rally. Things seem to be moving so fast already. Speaking of time—we need to get you to the gym for the ceremony."

"Can't wait to see what the kids think."

"Me neither." Amanda gestured, indicating that they were headed around the corner, toward the side wing of the school. "Let's go see."

Spencer couldn't stop pacing back and forth by the bleachers in the high school gym. In just a few minutes, months of Eve's hard work would come full circle and be turned over to the audience for which the art had been intended.

Full circle...Spencer paused and let his thoughts settle there. This year certainly had been a loop.

It wasn't that long ago that he'd stepped on the sand at Eve's beach house, demand letter from Mark in hand.

But it hadn't taken long to realize that linear path he'd been on wasn't the path to take him to his future. And thanks to Eve, he had a future.

This was the year he'd mended both his physical heart and his emotional one. And he had Eve to thank for both.

"Spencer! Good to see you, man." Dan Clark, the Port Provident High School head football coach, stopped and clapped Spencer on the shoulder. "I saw that Canley Investments signed on as a sponsor for the team this season. Really appreciate that."

"Happy to support the kids, Coach. Now, are we going to win the championship?" The local paper had covered upcoming season in this morning's edition and spoke highly of the Port Provident Pirates' chances of winning the coveted Texas high school football championship in their division.

"That's always the goal. This year's team is special. We just need to avoid distractions and stay focused the next few months."

"I'm sold. I'll be out at the game this weekend."

The coach smiled. "Glad to hear it. I'll see you out there. I've got to get in for the pep rally—but thanks again for the support this season."

"Anytime."

Within seconds of Coach Clark's departure, Spencer was back to pacing. He knew he needed to pick a spot up in the bleachers, sit down, and focus on the event and Eve.

But he couldn't.

Today was too important.

So, as the cheerleaders began to jump and stunt and the band began to strike up the fight song, Spencer moved down one set of bleachers so he could see Eve more clearly...then went right back to pacing.

An hour later, the football team was fired up and the students poured into the hallway, abuzz with chatter and the occasional shout.

Spencer looked for Eve and saw her walking out of the gym with Amanda Marsh and Lisa Fleming, who taught English and theater, respectively. The two teachers had provided a lot of thoughts and inspiration as Eve worked on the mural and a friendship had grown over the summer.

It made Spencer smile to see how easily things had come together this year for Eve. She'd started the year with tears, but as the year began to draw to a close, she had a new business, art commissions, friends...and a future with Spencer.

Or at least he'd hoped.

It was time to find out the answer for sure.

"Evie!" Spencer raised his voice to be heard over the commotion all around.

Eve shifted her path to head in Spencer's direction, and Amanda and Lisa followed behind. "I looked up in the bleachers, but I didn't see you. I'm so glad you made it."

Spencer shrugged at the recent memory of wearing a hole in the gymnasium floor. "I wasn't able to find a suitable place to sit. But the presentation was great. It was exciting to see Mayor Ruiz giving you a key to the city."

Eve's smile would have brightened the darkest night sky. "I wasn't expecting that! Such an honor. I love this town."

"Me too." Spencer placed a light kiss on Eve's cheek. "It took me a while to get here, but I don't plan to ever leave."

"Me neither. I hope I captured that in the mural."

Amanda chimed in. "I definitely think you did."

"Agree," said Lisa. "This is a special place and a special school—and anyone who sees this beautiful wall will know that just by looking at your art."

The four of them stood in front of the wall, studying the details as the crowd continued to filter through the hallway.

"Something isn't right." Spencer took a step back and made a face as he studied the mural.

"What?" A note of panic crept into Eve's voice. She looked back and forth. "Where, Spencer?

He pointed past the Shakespearean-style thatched roof that represented Amanda's classroom. "There, near that tree about two-thirds of the way down. Do you see it?"

Eve squinted as she studied the design on the wall. It made her nose wrinkle in the most adorable way. Spencer wished he could freeze this moment in time.

But if he did, he wouldn't be able to get to what would come next.

And although the nervous energy in his veins made him want to start pacing again, he wouldn't miss what was coming next for anything.

"What is that? It looks like gum or something. Who would put gum on your brand-new wall, Eve?" Lisa took a step closer.

Eve beat her to the spot in question, then studied it for a split second.

"It's not gum. It's a ball of clear tape of some kind. Ugh."

She began to pick at the edge of the tape with a fingernail. Spencer felt his own palms begin to sweat just a little bit.

"Wait a minute, there's something in here. It's not just trash." Eve picked at the semi-circle of tape a bit more.

"That's a ring," Amanda said, looking over Eve's shoulder.

Eve pulled it free of the tape and held it up. "It's a diamond ring. What on earth?"

The ring wasn't as big as the Kiss of Kiev or anything of historical significance.

But it had been bought with love and all the best of intentions.

Spencer took his cue and moved three steps forward, then sank to one knee in front of Eve. "This mural was missing something. You and me. And forever. Here. In our island, our town, our beach. The place we thought we'd use to get away from our problems—but instead turned out to be the key to our future. Eve Larson, this New Year's Eve, I want to be back on the beach with you—and a minister. Will you marry me?"

He held his breath for a split second. Eve looked at the ring in her hand. Her lips parted gently.

"Of course, Spencer. The answer is yes."

Amanda jumped up and down. "I just love love. It's the poetry teacher in me...but it just doesn't get any better than this."

Spencer stood and slid the ring on Eve's finger. "Actually, I plan to make every day to come better than the day before. I once told Eve that loving her was the best resolution I ever made. It's the truth. And it's a resolution I plan to make over and over again every single year."

You Don't Have to Leave Port Provident!

Start The Cupid Caper Now
Port Provident High School's favorite English teacher, Amanda Marsh, is in love with love and thrives on teaching her students classic love stories and sonnets—as she denies her own crush on science teacher Luke Baker. Continue the Holiday Hearts series and find out if matchmaking students at the school's Valentine's dance can make Cupid's arrow ring true...or if Amanda's secret dream of true love is destined to be another Shakespearean tragedy.
Start reading The Cupid Caper today!
www.books2read.com/TheCupidCaperBook

SOMETIMES YOU'VE GOT TO TAKE CUPID'S BOW AND ARROW INTO YOUR OWN HANDS...

Amanda Marsh is in love with love. As a high school English teacher, she is surrounded by poetry and classic literature, including the love stories written by her favorite author, William Shakespeare. She knows she'll never find anything as romantic as the stories that have stood the test of time, so she's settled on having a crush on chemistry teacher Luke Baker from afar

Luke Baker left behind his career as a research chemist in order to share a love of science with students. And he's about to make his pet project a reality as the curriculum lead for the district's new specialized science and technology academy. When a poen shows up on his desk drawing him into The Cupid Caper, the Valentine's Day-themed dance and fundraiser for Port Provident High School's Student Council, Luke dismisses the whole thing as a silly game. But after he realizes that winning the grand prize is the one way he can help a star student attend the new STEM Academy, he decides to play along.

Paired together, the hopeless romantic English teacher and the logical chemistry teacher both realize that The Cupid Caper is more than a game, but neither can tell the other their feelings are no joke.

When an education in happily-ever-after is on the line, will a man whose life has been ruled by the scientific method and a woman who quotes sonnets miss the mark, or will Cupid's arrow finally ring true?

If you're in love with sweet love stories that will make you smile as you swoon, The Cupid Caper is your perfect match.

www.books2read.com/TheCupidCaperBook

Join Kristen's Reader Community Today and Receive a Free Port Provident Story

Join Kristen's reader community today for the latest and get A Place to Find Love, *a sweet escape romance that introduces you to Port Provident, Texas and the residents who find love on the island, for free!*
www.kristenethridge.com/newsletter[1]

Sneak Peek: The Cupid Caper—Chapter One

"So, what are you going to do now that the cat's out of the bag?" Lisa Fleming leaned against the doorway of Amanda Marsh's classroom, her grin as feisty as another type of feline, the Cheshire Cat.

Amanda laid her red pen down and peered over the top of her glasses. "I have a thousand papers to grade before this weekend and you come to gossip?"

"Me? Gossip? I wouldn't dream of such a thing." Lisa feigned shock. "But tell me, Miss Shakespeare Teacher, what are you going to dream about when Luke Baker takes a leave of absence after Spring Break to go work on curriculum development for the new STEM Academy and then moves over there permanently next year?"

Port Provident ISD's new STEM Academy was the talk of the local education world. When it opened next fall, it would bring together the best teachers from across the district to teach Science, Technology, Engineering, and Mathematics to girls in a comprehensive format from Kindergarten through twelfth grade.

It would also take chemistry teacher Luke Baker away from the hallways of Port Provident High School and the daydreams of Port Provident's junior and senior level English teacher.

"I'm grading Lisa. Hush." She picked up her red pen. Maybe if she looked like she was focused on the piles of papers in front of her, Lisa would quit torturing her like a character from that *Mean Girls* movie.

"No you're not. That's *People* magazine on your desk. Not some AP test prep essay. You can't fool me." Lisa walked into Amanda's classroom and sat atop one of the desks in the back, near Amanda's own desk. "I know you got the email."

No use denying that. The announcement about the STEM Academy curriculum leads came out almost an hour ago, before the start of fourth period. "I did. And really, I'm happy for Luke. It's what he's wanted to do."

"Too bad all you've wanted to do for the past three years is go on a date with him."

"That is not accurate." Amanda could feel the tell-tale prickling in her cheeks, and knew she was beginning to blush the same color as the pen in her hand.

Lisa raised one eyebrow.

"It's only been two years," Amanda mumbled as she grabbed an essay off the pile at the corner of her desk. "He hasn't been at the school three years."

"Touché. My point still remains."

"I guess I'm going to do what anyone does when the—ahem—object of their affections moves on. I'll just move on too." Amanda tried to throw some sarcastic syllables in as she did her best to sound strong in her convictions. If she was honest with herself, she needed convincing far more than Lisa did. "Besides, you know I am just not in to that whole dating scene. There are no more fairy tales anymore."

"Really?" Lisa drew out the syllables. Amanda knew she was being baited.

"You know it and I know it. So, do you have any better ideas?"

"As a matter of fact, I do." Lisa stood up and pointed to the hand-painted poster from Student Council on the back wall. "You're just going to have to do what every other girl in this school is doing for the next week. The Cupid Caper."

"The Cupid Caper? Really, Lisa. I'm not eighteen. And I'm not participating in some secret Valentine scavenger hunt type thing—I mean, what is it, really, anyway?—to ask Luke Baker to a high school dance." The blush dropped from her cheeks like the mercury in a thermometer pelted by a cold front. "I should have known the resident drama teacher would have some kind of so-called solution with absolutely no basis in reality."

Lisa quickly closed the gap between her and the teacher's desk as she talked.

"Look, Amanda. Being the drama teacher means I can see through people's masks. I know when someone's pretending. And you're pretending like you don't care that Luke is leaving in a matter of a few weeks." She placed her hands squarely on the fake wood grain top of her best friend's desk. "Pretending poorly, I might add. You certainly aren't going to win an Oscar with this performance."

"I don't want to win an Oscar. I might like to win a date with Luke Baker. And still keep my dignity. But if I have to choose, I'll take my dignity every time."

Amanda looked at the industrial clock on the wall, narrow black hand marking the passage of each second. *Was her conference period over yet?*

Some break this was. Amanda coveted the thirty minutes of peace and quiet she got in the middle of each school day. Usually she filled the time with grading or polishing lesson plans. But the key was always peace and quiet.

Not today.

"I know you think I'm crazy. But you've had a crush on this guy for years, and now he's taking a new job at a new school. If you don't do something, you'll never see him again. Don't you think you ought to do *something*?"

Maybe Lisa was right. But if she made the wrong move, the gossip would spread like wildfire through the hallways of Port Provident High. And if there was anything more stressful than teaching about one-hundred-and-twenty seventeen- and eighteen-year-olds to love literature that wasn't necessarily on their Kindle, it was trying to teach those one-hundred-and-twenty seventeen-and eighteen-year-olds while they were laughing at her.

"I just don't think The Cupid Caper is the right answer. I know all the kids have a lot of fun with it, but I'm a teacher. It would be silly."

Lisa continued leaning over the desk, invading Amanda's personal space. Clearly, she thought she knew best, and she wasn't giving up. "Linda and Bob do The Cupid Caper every year, so there's precedent. Besides, insanity is defined as doing the same thing the same way and expecting different results, right?"

"Linda and Bob have been married for more than thirty years." The two math teachers were close to retirement and the unofficial grandparents to almost every teenager who walked the halls of Port Provident High. "And yes, it is. I tell my students that often."

"So..." A bright gleam twinkled in Lisa's eye. Amanda knew grand plans swirled in her best friend's head. And she knew she'd have to do some quick thinking to get them diffused. "Sometimes you just have to take Cupid's bow and arrow into your own hands."

"Dr. Baker?" The other students had raced out of the room when the final bell for the day rang, but Violet Clark lingered near the doorway.

"What's up, Violet?" Luke Baker pinched the center ring of a three-ring binder closed, then looked up at the shy girl with the dark curls.

"Is it true that you're leaving?" Apprehension spread clearly across her face. From the furrowed brow, to the dark stare, to the gentle chew on her lower lip, it was clear she'd heard the news somewhere—and it wasn't sitting well.

Although the announcement had been made to only faculty and staff a few periods before, it didn't surprise Luke one bit that word had gotten out to the kids. Information was the key commodity in the halls of any high school. Traded more furiously than stocks on Wall Street, there were no secrets that could be kept long.

"It's true. I'm headed to the new STEM Academy."

"But they said you're leaving before the year is over." The volume level of Violet's voice dialed sharply downward.

Luke could have kicked himself. In all the excitement of getting the call notifying him of his new position, he'd glossed over the part about telling his students. Most of them wouldn't necessarily care too much. Teachers came and teachers went. These kids rotated between seven classes a day. They were used to change, and as a whole, kids were resilient.

But still, there were some for whom attachments ran deep. And Violet Clark was one of them. The only child of a single mom who worked two jobs, Violet had blossomed in the chemistry lab. She'd found a world of rules and order, where things always made sense. A place where the giants like Marie Curie inspired young scientists even today with the promise of discovery.

And now, Violet had made a discovery which would change a very important corner of the world—the only secure corner she really possessed.

"Well, I don't know who *they* are..." Luke hesitated just a bit, wondering if he should try and soften it or just come out and lay out the truth. "But that's right. There will be a long-term sub in here after Spring Break. I'm being sent back to school in a way, myself. I'll be taking some courses that pertain to curriculum development. Then I'm going to spend most of the summer heading up the committee to bring together the curriculum we'll be using at the STEM Academy."

Violet nodded. "Can I come with you?"

Luke fiddled with the pen in his hand. He wasn't quite sure where she was going with this. "Where?"

"The STEM Academy."

Of course, Luke. The school. He needed to quit listening to the women in the teachers' lounge talking about students having crushes on teachers and all that stuff. Besides, Violet wasn't that type. If he didn't know himself better, he'd wonder if he'd been sniffing chemicals from the back cabinet of his chemistry lab.

"Well, there's an application process." Seeing the serious look that crossed her face, Luke made a decision. Violet was the type of girl who the STEM Academy catered to. Her whole life could be changed with exposure to the sciences and the higher-paying jobs she could have access to after college. "I'll print out a copy for you and we can work on the application together. There are some essays too."

Violet gave a shy smile. Luke felt good about making the offer. He'd spent time with a drug manufacturer before walking away to teach. No patent, no accolade, nothing in his former career gave him the same satisfaction as seeing the spark in a student's eyes.

"Maybe Miss Marsh could help me with those. Do you think she would?"

Luke wanted to say yes, but he didn't really know. Amanda Marsh always seemed to have a full plate. The students loved her English classes, and when she didn't have her nose in one of the classics, she was running to Student Council meetings or working with the drill team. There were twenty-four hours in every day, and as best he could tell, Amanda Marsh scurried through every single one of them.

Quite frankly, he'd never seen the lights in her classroom off when he walked to his car—even late at night. He assumed she kept a futon in the back corner not for students to read, but so she could just sleep there and never leave.

"You could always ask her, Violet."

"I'll have to remember to do it tomorrow. I'm going to miss the bus if I don't hurry."

Luke gestured with his hands, a pushing motion toward the hallway. "Don't miss the bus. The applications aren't due for another two weeks. We'll get it taken care of."

"Ok Dr. Baker. Thanks." Violet adjusted her backpack on her shoulders and turned to walk through the doorway. "I'll see you tomorrow."

"No problem, Violet. See you tomorrow."

Luke walked down the quiet hallway toward the doors which led to the teachers' parking lot at the back of the building. School ended about ninety minutes before, and without the jam-packed bustle of teenagers, Port Provident High seemed more in line with his old life at a corporate giant. People kept to themselves, just trying to finish the last of the day's work so they could go home.

The students gave the walls and halls their heart, and even though Luke believed deeply in the order and rules of chemistry and the sciences, he knew the energy he got from these kids more than made up for what was missing out of his paycheck these days.

He could see the light on in the room at the end of the hallway. A faux thatched roof poked out from over the doorway and construction paper timbers framed it. Amanda Marsh took her responsibility to literature seriously—down to decorating the entrance to her classroom to resemble Shakespeare's Globe Theatre.

Since she was still here, Luke decided to walk through the entrance to Shakespeare World and ask about the application essays on Violet's behalf. That way they could start working on them as soon as possible.

"Amanda? You got a minute?" Luke opened the door quietly and stepped inside.

A Tiffany-style lamp sat on the corner of Amanda's desk. It put a soft glow on her head, bent low tending to some of her grading. The light fell softly and gave her red hair highlights that sparkled like they could be measured in karats.

Amanda Marsh was one of those teachers everyone talked about—in a good way. Luke had always thought she was a bit scatterbrained, but as she lifted her head, light gray-green eyes upturned and a smattering of freckles across the bridge of her nose, Luke took a hard look at her.

And that look hit him hard right back, a punch to the gut.

It made him swallow hard, a roughness like sandpaper sliding down his throat. He'd worked with her for two years and had always thought of her as being Port Provident's own personal Lucy Ricardo.

Maybe he'd been wrong to stereotype her. Those eyes were serious, studying the words in front of her with intensity. And that hair. Soft, layered gently over her shoulders, and sassy.

Cut it out, Baker. He'd come in here to ask a favor from a colleague on behalf of a student. Not to ask the English teacher out on a date.

"Sure. What's up?" She'd looked up, but spoke before she really noticed who she was talking to. Her eyes flicked up to Luke's face, then immediately darted down toward the papers scattered across the desktop.

Scratch all that earlier stuff. The English teacher definitely was a scatterbrain. She couldn't even sustain eye contact.

"Hey, Violet Clark is in one of your classes, right?" He decided to stay back by the door. If scatterbrained-ness was catching, he didn't want to come down with a case. Luke was pretty sure none of his former colleagues back at Global Health were researching a vaccine for over-taxed synapse disorder.

Amanda lifted her head back and appeared to be squaring her jaw, as though she was fighting her way through something distasteful. Luke wished he'd never stopped by. He had a few degrees and some letters after his name that he didn't have much use for in a high school setting—sure they were in chemistry, but he'd had to write both a thesis and a dissertation. It wasn't like he didn't grasp the basics of the English language. Maybe he should just help Violet with the essays too.

"She's in my Advanced Placement English III class. Why do you ask?"

Luke decided to just throw it all out there bluntly, and get this over with. "She's expressed an interest in applying to the STEM Academy. I told her I'd help her with the overall application, but that there were some essays. She thought you might be able to review those for her."

Her ring finger tapped in a non-sensical pattern atop the stack of papers. "Sure. Violet's one of my best students in that class, though. I doubt she'll need much help."

"She's a good kid—does well in my class also. That's why I told her I'd help. I'll have her stop by once she's finished the essays. Should be later this week."

Luke turned to walk out the door, but before he could get back to the hallway, Amanda called out.

"Luke?" Her high, clear voice cut through the silence in the classroom like a diamond on glass.

He pivoted on the ball of his foot. "What?"

"The STEM Academy isn't exactly close to here. Violet's mother works too many hours to transport her over there. And they can't afford a car for Violet, even though I know she got her license last spring. Even if she got in to the new school, how will she get there every day?"

The nervousness on her face fell away, replaced with the soft shades of concern. Her lips fell a shade more pale, the freckles muted their orange shine, and the irises of her eyes shifted from mostly green to an overcast gray.

Clearly, Amanda Marsh cared as deeply for the quiet girl from the disadvantaged background as much as Luke himself did. He understood why. The young woman was a dream student: curious, conscientious, and respectful. Not every kid possessed those qualities in combination these days. Most had one or two, but the seasoned teachers around the halls said they wished they could teach one hundred Violet Clarks.

"You know," Luke said slowly, trying to think of something he could do to change the reality of the situation. "I don't know, Amanda."

She raked a hand through her shiny hair and let out a deep breath. "I love the idea of the STEM Academy, but I worry about kids like Violet who would thrive in that environment—but can't get there. I'm just not sure we're doing the right thing as a district. Maybe we should have focused on creating programs within the existing schools."

"I think the STEM Academy is still the right move." He tried not to be defensive, but he took the STEM Academy personally. He'd been one of the key employees in the district backing this project. If the STEM Academy failed students before even getting off the ground—well, it was like *he* failed students.

And he didn't get into teaching to fail his students.

"I'm sure it is. Even this English teacher thinks a place with a higher focus on science and math and those career paths is a great idea. I just worry about the kids like Violet—all of the talent to really benefit from it—but lacking the support and resources to make the transition."

Luke nodded. He felt like he was reassuring himself as much as the English teacher. "It'll work."

Keep reading The Cupid Caper

Click here: www.books2read.com/TheCupidCaperBook

The Holiday Hearts Series

The Right Resolution[1]
The Cupid Caper[2]
Lucky in Love[3]
The Bachelor and the Easter Bunny[4]
May I Have This Dance[5]
First Kiss Fireworks[6]
Falling Forever This Time[7]
Thankful for Love[8]
Mission: Mistletoe[9]

Want to extend your stay in Port Provident?
Start reading the Hearts and Hope Series
Shelter from the Storm[10]

---

1. http://www.books2read.com/TheRightResolutionBook

2. http://www.books2read.com/TheCupidCaperBook

3. http://www.books2read.com/LuckyInLoveBook

4. http://www.books2read.com/BachelorAndEasterBunnyBook

5. http://www.books2read.com/MayIHaveThisDanceBook

6. http://www.books2read.com/FirstKissFireworksBook

7. http://www.books2read.com/FallingForeverThisTimeBook

8. http://www.books2read.com/ThankfulForLoveBook

9. http://www.books2read.com/MissionMistletoeBook

The Doctor's Unexpected Family[11]
His Texas Princess[12]
Holiday of Hope[13]

Other Books by Kristen

Love Hallmark movies? Pick up Kristen's book October Kiss, based on the Hallmark movie viewers love! Available anywhere books are sold—in paperback, digital, and audio! October Kiss from Hallmark Publishing[14]

---

10. http://www.books2read.com/ShelterFromTheStorm

11. http://www.books2read.com/TheDoctorsUnexpectedFamily

12. http://www.books2read.com/HisTexasPrincess

13. http://www.books2read.com/HolidayOfHope

14. https://www.books2read.com/OctoberKiss

About Kristen

K risten Ethridge writes Sweet Escape Romance—stories with hope, heart and happily-ever-after—for Harlequin's Love Inspired line, Hallmark Publishing, and Laurel Lock Publishing. She's a Romance Writers of America Golden Heart Award nominee and both a Christian Fiction and Inspirational Romance #1 Best-Selling Author.

You can find Kristen in her native habitat—a Texas patio—where she's likely to be savoring the joy of a crispy taco, along with a glass of iced tea. Scents from her essential oil diffuser are also a must, since she's a certified aromatherapist. She's almost convinced her family that it's normal to talk to imaginary people, as long it goes in a book.

Find her online at http://www.kristenethridge.com where you can get a free story for signing up for her newsletter. You can also follow her adventures in writing at www.facebook.com/kristenethridgebooks[1].

Keep up with Kristen by joining her newsletter list[2] and her author pages on Bookbub[3] and Facebook[4]. If you can't get enough of Port Provident, come join the Port Provident Reader Society[5] on Facebook, the official gathering place for Kristen and her fans.

www.kristenethridge.com[6]

Facebook[7] Instagram[8]

The Port Provident Reader Society[9]

Don't forget...if you love sweet escape romances, join Kristen's newsletter[10]!

---

1. http://www.facebook.com/kristenethridgebooks

2. http://www.kristenethridge.com/newsletter

3. https://www.bookbub.com/authors/kristen-ethridge

4. http://www.facebook.com/kristenethridgebooks

5. https://www.facebook.com/groups/2422381554654795

6. http://www.kristenethridge.com

7. https://www.facebook.com/KristenEthridgeBooks

8. https://instagram.com/kristenethridge

9. https://www.facebook.com/groups/2422381554654795

10. http://www.kristenethridge.com

Acknowledgements

Being a writer means working alone. But thankfully, I'm not always talking to myself. To my crew who has listened to me A LOT over the past two months or so, thank you for saving what's left of my sanity. I love calling you friends and talking about all the crazy stuff that makes being a writer equally great and frustrating.

Thank you, Elana Johnson, Danica Favorite, and Kat Cantrell for being you, being awesome, and being there.

"Because of the Lord's great love, we are not
consumed, for his compassions never fail. They are
new every morning; great is your faithfulness."
—LAMENTATIONS 3:22-23 (NIV)

Laurel Lock Publishing

Publisher's Note: This is a work of fiction. Names, characters, places, and incidents are a product of the author's imagination. Locales and public names are sometimes used for atmospheric purposes. Any resemblance to actual people, living or dead, or to businesses, companies, events, institutions, or locales is completely coincidental.

---

1.   http://www.zondervan.com/

www.ingramcontent.com/pod-product-compliance
Lightning Source LLC
Chambersburg PA
CBHW030341180626
46812CB00007B/2719